AF190793

My nightly wanderings

under shining stars

and darken sky

My nightly wanderings under shining stars and darken skies

Copyright Henrik Neergaard, 2020.

Published by Books-on-Demand, Copenhagen, Denmark

Printed by Books-on-Demand, Norderstedt, Germany

ISBN 9788743016267

Henrik Neergaard

My Nightly Wanderings Under Shining Stars and Darken Skies

BoD

Books-on-Demand

FSC
www.fsc.org

MIX

Papir fra
ansvarlige kilder
Paper from
responsible sources

FSC® C105338

Chapter 1

Where, among other things, I make a bet that I get some problems with

It's all Mona's fault. Well, that's it. Certainly. That is beyond doubt. Simply. She's the one who's responsible for all this. She's the one who made me do it, or, it was actually her sister. But it was Mona who invited me to that gathering, where her sister was also with her, and it was here, that is, her sister, who enticed me to make that bet.

Okay, I guess I wasn't completely sober either. Maybe I was even pretty drunk. I have to admit that. It was a Christmas get-together, and it was already past midnight. So why shouldn't I be drunk? She was pretty drunk herself. We all were.

Otherwise, I would never have agreed to a bet like that. I was even stupid enough to bet the whole of $1,000 when she kept challenging me and said I probably couldn't. I mean, write a book. Of course I could do that! Just as well as anyone else. Of course I can! But she kept saying me that I couldn't. And that it's only academics like herself who can write books.

But that's bullshit. I can do that, too, I said. And then she challenged me to that bet. So now I'm hanging on to it.

And now I'm going to get started. It's probably just going to be some of the things from my daily life, which I'm going to take a look at and then just embroider a little bit, maybe. Kind of a diary, maybe with a few extra curls on it. Something like that. But I guess that should be okay, too. Then it is quite reminiscent of what is known as autofiction, which I think is one of the hottest among many writers at the moment. At least she says so. Mona's sister. So now I'm starting that writing. I don't really know what it's going to be like. I'm actually quite excited about it myself. But then it's their fault. Mona and her sister who lured me into this. But I'm sure going to find something to put into this book. It can't be that difficult.

Chapter 2

Where the action gets going. At least I'm counting on that.

Okay, here we go. I don't want to write the date. It's not a real diary after all. One of those where you have to write something every day. Whether you have experienced something exciting or not. I don't want to do that. Then it gets too boring. And I'm going to have time for something other than this.

So now I'm trying. I'm going to take out my good will. I'm looking at it a little bit, wondering what am I going to do with it right now. I'll get some kind of idea. I'm going to throw my good will into the midnight hour. Like it's a closet I'm throwing it into, maybe. Maybe a wardrobe, clothes create people, they say. Or maybe it's some kind of storeroom. Some kind of warehouse of something. A warehouse filled with good will, perhaps. Or just with a lot of words and letters. Or thoughts that can be written down. It's always nice to have something in stock for worse times. Save some good will for a rainy day, as they say.

A grey and sour day when everything goes against you. Then it is very good to have such a few small depots of good will lying around that one can draw on. That's why I always finance my good will a little when it's there, so you don't prey on it. It is always essential to have it promoted. You don't have to overdraft the account, either.

Yes, I do know that some people say that the one who saves for the night saves for the night. No, nonsense, I mean, the one who saves for the night saves for the cat. It can be a little hard to keep track of things like this in the wolf class just after midnight. yes, I'm talking about the good old wolf class. And not just some hasty shopping on the way home from work, some stressful cooking and some picky, untidy pups to be fed off. This is how everything is trivialised in modern society. And then, at all, will not begin to comment on why that expression with the wolf class has changed meaning and what it says about society today. I don't give up on that kind of thing, because it's not the time or the times.

I'm a little busy getting to grips with this weird, quirky and unruly hour that just soars between night and day. Or to be correct, of course it is between day and night, and not between night and day. yes, this is the wolf class I'm still talking about. This no-man's land, where the energy of the day is running out and the energy of the night has not really come into gear.

But by the way, I don't believe in hiding for the cat at all. I don't keep a cat at all, so there's no cat to hide anything for. I don't want to feed the neighbor's cat.

So I'm not hiding anything for the cat. I'm not hiding anything for the night, either. I don't. I'm just not saving my good will for the night. I'm not saving it for the night. On the contrary, I save it FOR the night. I'll hide it away in a safe place. Almost as if I had a safe deposit box. Lock and strike in some kind of mental safe. So that it does not be captured and over-penetrated and corrupted by the night and all its being. Such! Or what if I dropped it out in the city? In fact, it's easy to get to that. Especially if you are in town at night and it has become rather late and you also have had a bit to drink.

I think I'll leave my good intentions at home. It should preferably be intact, so I can take it out of the closet again sometime tomorrow morning. Experience tells me that very often, the morning after a night like this, where you may have been a little bit of a lot around town, you might actually need a great deal of really good intentions.

A little break. I'll pour myself a little whiskey. Just one.

Just. One. Small. Whiskey.

Time for a bit of thinking before I go ahead with the deeds of the night.

Then I walk into the room next door and to the old black-painted closet. It's a bit of a horror, certainly not pretty to look at. Quite a scuffled, and not even very practical. So I don't really know why I keep it, that's what I inherited after Uncle Rufus. He was actually called that. yes, okay, maybe he was a bit of a dog, and cheeky like a butcher dog. So maybe the name fit very well. He was also a dog after fast cars and naughty ladies and colorful drinks and all that sort of thing, but otherwise......... Well, I think that goes too far, this. But I can safely say that, compared to him, I am almost a total pattern of virtue.

Yet he bequeathed me a big closet full of old magazines and stuff like that. Or maybe that's exactly why. At least I prefer to believe that. That sounds nicer than the opposite. But it was a little embarrassing that it was actually in his will, black and white. And I had said yes to the thing of confessing to inheritance and debt, because I thought he had a great deal of money saved up, because that had been talked about, and I could also remember that he had had that in the past. But it turned out that he had sunned it all up, so all he left behind was that ugly old closet with its more or less obscene content. That's the way it can go.

When I got the closet, it was both locked with a regular lock and with two difficult padlocks. And it was an explicit condition that I only opened it once I had the closet transported home to myself. He had even written me a rather long and almost entirely touching letter. Or a very sentimental one, at least. A real old-fashioned handwritten letter with his distinctive handwriting. The letter said a whole lot of phrases and piping about all the valuable things that were in the closet and which he believed would enrich my life. I thought this was where he had hidden a fortune in money or valuables or shares or a rare stamp collection or something like that. But I was so badly disappointed. There was nothing but about half a ton of old worn and curly magazines and bang novels and stuff like that. I didn't know anything about that beforehand. But all the locals up there in Northern Jutland, where he lived, knew what was in his big black closet. And for some reason, almost everyone in the village had turned up to the local event, where his will was to be opened at the lawyer's office. And when the lawyer opened the will and read out with a loud and clear voice that I, his only nephew, would inherit the great black closet with all its content, a quiet giggle began to spread among all the locals, without me initially understanding why. I only discovered this when I had the old closet transported home and had the locks broken up. I think this was his last attempt to educate me a little bit. Or so he might have thought with his crooked mind.

But after all, I sort of liked him. I salute him with one more J.O.S.W. – Just. One. Small. Whisky.

Chapter 3

I don't just bother reading an old bang novel and instead I find out a bit about my night's will

Well, the first real chapter was perfectly good, I think. Kind of naughty and a little nice language and such. It's coming along, I think. So now I'm going to move on.

Now the closet is no longer full of all those old magazines and cheap bang novels. The old black closet that I inherited from Uncle Rufus. I'm using it for some other stuff now. Worse or better, it might be a matter of taste. But now I'm getting ready.

Carefully, I open the one door of the large cupboard. Almost with a kind of awe. For out comes my night will, as I call it. It's the easiest thing to call it, and it sounds pretty neutral. Close to just being a word, a name that one – ie I – has put on it, almost in line with if it was a chair or a table.

A neutral statement. Almost as if it's your nightwear you put on, for example. And it's almost a kind of nightwear that I wear. Although it is not exactly a pajamas, but something a little more deep black, festive and, in a sense, I would also say rather more colourful than that. All in a transferred sense, of course. Because at night, all cats are black-grey, at least as long as they stay out in the dark of night and the moon is not there. Only when they enter the floodlights do you see their colors and patterns. If they're someone worth talking about.

But here after midnight, I put my night's will on, and nothing gets to hang loose. Not until later in the night. But for now, it's a different story. Now I just put my night's will, freshly stroked and smooth-brushed. There's nothing going on about that, as they say. As someone says. I can just take it off again, right? And it doesn't have to be right at sunrise. Because I'm not a vampire, am I? Of course I'm not! I can wear all night, if I want, until the morning, or well into the morning, if it suits me.

It's all going very well, I can feel it. I believe in this thing with my good will hidden in a safe place, almost like in a safe deposit box, so I can take it back out on Monday. If I haven't lost the key out in town. Or if a pickpocket of some kind has seen his cut to nail it in the night. One never knows.

But now at least the roulette is running again. Ladies and gentlemen, make your bets! Red or black? Think of a number! Choose for yourself! Make a decision! How much do you want to bet? Rien ne vas plus!

And the wheel of the roulette spins again. I wonder where it's going to land this time.

Chapter 4

Where not much happens, I'm afraid

I've got up early, way too soon. It's only five o'clock in the morning! I'm yawning. I'm going to scribscrap. I'm freezing. I need to shake the remnants of sleep off me. And i haven't even slept enough. I was way late to bed. And then the fucking alarm clock. It really fucked me. I must have come to put it wrong. I really hate that kind of thing.

I don't think it's one of my very best mornings. And now there's a big breadcrumb that's gone down in my coffee and swelled to huge size. Shut up, it's disgusting. I'm going to start fishing it up with a teaspoon. I don't want breadcrumbs in my coffee. But now there's a lot of coffee on the table. And the breadcrumb is still there. Oh,. I pour the coffee into the sink and pour myself a new cup. Without breadcrumbs in it.

I'll take a big sip of the coffee. And a little less sip. And another one. I'm going to get up and put on an extra sweater. Maybe I shouldn't have gotten up yet. Maybe I should have waited a few hours.

A false start. That's just what it is. A false start of the day. It usually doesn't work very well. Maybe I should just go back to bed. Lie and put me under the down. But now I've become awake. I'm a little restless, I can feel. I have a headache, too. I probably should have taken some earlier home.

I look at the clock very carefully. Want to make sure I'm not wrong. But no, it's still only half six. Such a time when I should still be sleeping rough under the duvet. Especially when I'm not going up and going to work or anything. It's week-end. Silly idea to wake up so early. Why did I get to mess with that alarm clock that last night, totally silly.

I'll turn on the radio. But there's nothing interesting. Besides, it's making too much noise. It makes my headache even worse. I'm going to have to turn it off again.

I yawn loudly. And one more time. I'm heavy in the head. So the thoughts are a little sluggish. Almost as if my brain is resisting being used right now. Like it'd rather just be at peace, without having to figure anything out. Maybe I should go back to bed after all.

Yes, yes, the first ones are going to be the last, and all that, you start by getting up early, then you go back to bed and sleep over, so you end up getting too late.

Especially if you have to do something. Do you know the type?

No, it doesn't matter. I'm not in the mood to play philosopher or professor or schoolteacher right now. I need some more coffee. To wake up right on. I need that. Maybe I should eat something, too. Some breakfast for example. Some real breakfast. But I don't really want to.

I just want to have a good time and have a good time and have it all served. Just like last night, it was pretty cool. It's not the first time that We've got to do that.

Isn't this cold? Why am I just sitting here freezing? Pull yourself together and do something, man! Get some time together! Do something sensible! I'm trying to incite myself a little bit. I'm thinking about the idea, anyway.

yes, yes, in a minute. I'm yawning again. Deeply and fervently. Then I'll go and pour that cup of coffee that I was thinking of a few minutes ago. Better late than never. I don't want to risk wasting slowly and carefully. I'm hardly shaking my hand. I'm really concentrating on the task. Be careful, don't waste.

Gently, gently. Well, actually, it succeeded very well. And then a decent square sugar. It all helps. I'm going to stir and take a sip of the hot coffee. And one more.

Oh, that's great. Just what I need. I'll take another sip. But I'm still freezing. I get up and go and turn up the heat. I'm going to pull the curtain aside a little bit and look out. It doesn't look very welcoming. Grey and cloudy. But at least now it's getting bright.

Chapter 5

That's the one where I don't meet a diesel chick after all.

I wonder what time it is. Ten minutes to seven! Damn it, time's up! I have to go, I'm late for work. Why can't I take care of time. It's a because of last night. I know. But it's not that simple when you're in the middle of it, it's not everything you can plan for in advance. Then it would also be hugely boring. There can be as much as you want to follow up on along the way. That's just what happened there last night, but of course it would be nice enough if you could control it a little more.

I know I promised myself I'd go home by 2:00. But that kind of thing doesn't always last. It was just because it all worked out so well. The atmosphere was perfectly okay, and so with a little on top. Just as it should be. And then there was that one, the handsome redhead. That's a little bit why, too.

She looked even better than she used to. And then that blouse. But those three guys she was with all the time, they were just some disgusting types. They made themselves quite strange. These were the kind of people you didn't really bother to be friends with, and then there were three of them, all three with quite large muscles. I don't understand why she wants to be around these types.

So I stayed in the background for a while. But I was waiting for these guys to leave so I could get her a little more for myself. And then maybe I stayed there a little too long.

Because it didn't work out the way I'd bet. They didn't go, those three idiots. They kept staying there. I don't know what happened to her. It looked like she almost didn't care about anyone but them, but I didn't want to just give up, would I? So I stayed there until they closed. And I should have a drink in the meantime.

None of the other women's ladies were really interesting. Not exactly my type. There was, of course, Suzzie, she even came and sat down at my table, totally dyed and everything. It's been a while since, after all. She'd even got a new marker, but it was just such a weird rubbed crime. And then, of course, she had set herself this way, so she just sat in the way of the prospect of Jeanette, that is, her the redhead. It was probably on purpose.

But I don't really want to do that anymore. So Suzzie, of course. Now it's some other kind of song. I used to be there. For a shorter period of time, it must be said. But she can be quite annoying sometimes. Not to be counted on.

Then you might as well start lying in with one of those bleached and overly silicone-spat diesel shafts out from the cafeteria by the bypass. Out there at the rest stop where the truckers are holding in for lunch and going to the toilet and everything else. But that's just not my style at all.

Suzzie isn't that bad after all. Not as far as I know anyway. Right, but you never really know. But I talked to her a little bit anyway. Just not to be rude and not to sit and bore me. And of course also, because I was a little curious to hear what she had been doing lately. Just to stay up to date on it, you can always use that. She had just been let down by some bastard here recently. He had just left her, she said. And she had really bet that it was going to be the two. So she felt lonely and abandoned and needed a lot for some company. She made absolutely no secret of that.

I actually sat and started to consider her a little when the time started to get many and Jeanette still wasn't to come near. Just for old friendship's sake, and because Maybe I was a little sentimental after all. We'd had some good things together sometimes. But I just had to weigh a little for and against. It could well be that she was also on such a small non-committal thing. On the other hand, she can also be a little sticky if you get too well layered with her. Nor is it always good to return to something that once was. So I just had to clarify with myself.

I set and paddled the conversation a little while I tried to think. But then I decided to try anyway. But just when I was about to run loose with some more purposeful scoring, she suddenly got up and went out the back with some guy who had just come up to here and had exchanged a dozen short sentences with her. It sounded like they already knew each other. I don't know where they went. At least she didn't come back. And Jeanette was still drinking and laughing and having fun with those three types, laughing at their stupid jokes apparently and not minding them set and raging at here. In the end, she started to rage a little on him, too. Or not just a little, actually. It was really disgusting to watch.

It was a real bad night. And the night too, and now it's a real bad morning. Where I even have to go to work. . But it's no good turning me in sick again. They've seen that too many times.

Chapter 6

Where I don't get to read that book about them "Holy Hookers from the Jungle" either – the ones that conquer the government, and that's just because...

Peeling onions. Peeling onions. Peeling more onions. Peeling off the outer brown layers. Slowly and carefully. Or quickly to get it over with so it doesn't stitch in the eyes longer than necessary.

Maybe also in a transferred sense, if you start to think about things. Or play a little psychologist with himself. You have to be careful about that.

But then the onions have to be cooked too. To make them into something edible. Or even delicious.That's the point. There are many ways to do it. Raw onions. Some like them raw, chopped onions like that. To go with a hot dog, for example. If you are at a good old hot dog stand.

Or onion rings. Still raw. For a herring food maybe.

Or fried onions. Soft onions. Or black-boned onions. If they've had a little too much. Or roasted onions. One of the classics. The ones you buy in such a small plastic tub at Netto. If you do. If you eat that kind of thing. I think that's a little bit on the way out. Someone says it's not onions they're made of at all, but chopped white cabbage or something. But I don't know if it's true. I'm sure it won't. People say so much nonsense. I don't usually eat that kind of thing anyway. Only once in a while.

There are also pickled onions. Some small ones in a glass with a pickle in some variety. Pearl onions, they're called. Suzzie liked to get in all sorts of stews. She almost always did. Both made stews and put those little silly pearl onions in, and often with peas, for some reason. She did that almost every time they were the ones who cooked. She probably had a rather old-fashioned idea of food. When I was in charge of it, it was either steaks or lasagna or meat sauce spaghetti or once pizza. Someone who just needed a ride in the above. Why make it more difficult than it needs to be.

No, this is silly. I don't want to fill my book like that, but what am I going to do?

Yes, Now I know that old closet that I inherited from my uncle. There was a lot of old curly magazines and some old bang novels at the bottom of the closet and on some of the shelves. Apparently, that was the kind of thing he liked to read. There was some funny stuff in between. For example, this old bang novel, which was at the top of the stack, and which, incidentally, lacks some pages. I don't think it would work out today. The drawing on the cover is like real primitive, and it's called "Holy Hookers from the Jungle". Just think about that title! It's a real sleazy bang novel from when my uncle was young. It was one of those I didn't really bother reading that other night.

It takes place somewhere in Africa where there is some civil war or unrest, and one side is assisted by some white mercenaries from South Africa who are attacking a monastery with some nuns who then...........

Oh no, now my phone rings. It's Soren who's going to complain about something. He always does. I think this time it's something about a new girlfriend who doesn't really bother about him anyway. It's not the first time. I've heard that story before. Or he's complaining about something else. But I owe him some money, so I had better try to be nice and understanding. For a couple of minutes, at least.

Chapter 7

Where I start reading that book about the holy hookers from the jungle anyway

So, where did I get to before he called? Just a minute, I will just grab a beer in the fridge, and turn on some music. Okay, I'm ready.

Yes, that's the thing about my uncle's old novel. That one about these holy hookers somewhere in Africa. As I was beginning to say, it's about a monastery run by some missionaries somewhere in the jungle or in the bush, getting involved in a civil war or some unrest where the fronts wave back and forth.

There is also a kind of convent school, a kind of high school, where some missionaries will give young local women some form of higher education. There are about 180 young women at the school, which is a boarding school run by the nuns and some priests at the monastery itself.

The riots waves back and forth, and one day some white mercenaries come to the convent school.

And then the next few chapters are missing. So I don't know what happens after that.

But now it's also getting food time, and I can feel that I'm really well hungry. So something has to be done about that. I don't know why I'm going to think of those stews again. The ones that Suzzie always made. It got a little monotonous. I'm sure it was healthy and everything. She always poured a lot of vegetables in. Not until afterwards. I guess I didn't treat her very nicely. But it was only afterwards that I could see it for myself. I think I almost let her go for lye and cold water, as they say. But it was also because I was so intoxicated by her the blonde. Marianne.

Or not drunk. I was really captivated by her. I was. Or maybe a little drunk, anyway. With her, too. A lot of the time.

She wasn't very good at cooking. Not much better than me. But we didn't really care about that, at least at first. We had other things to think about. But sooner or later, it usually comes a little more on the agenda. The only thing she was really good at, that is, about cooking, was to fry some good juicy steaks with lots of soft onions. There it was again, the one with the onions.

It was a bit old fashioned maybe, but she was the best at it in the whole block. She just didn't always bother.

She'd had enough of it when she had that job of standing and making old-fashioned steak sandwiches with soft onions and the whole mess in some steak joint inside Tivoli. That's when she learned it, and that's why she was so good at it.

Well, that was a digression. It's just because I'm hungry. And there's nothing in the fridge. I didn't get to buy in yesterday. I'd better call for a pizza or something.

Chapter 8

Where I try to be just a little bit of a poet

I need some fresh air. And to stretch my legs. Move about a little. I'm going to go for a walk.

I'm going out in the dark. Night has fallen, it's late, actually. The clouds drift across the sky, and the moon glows when the clouds allow it. It sounds almost a little poetic, doesn't it? But it's cold and it's blowing. There's almost no traffic. Nor any other night walkers. Not right here. It's also a pretty quiet neighborhood. Okay, it's probably not very poetic after all.

But I don't give up so easily. Now it's the clouds that rule, and we're down here freezing a little under a hideous orange-lit street lamp. The world is filled with orange-colored lights. Warning flashes. Watch out, watch out. Rotating orange lights on every other truck that keeps quiet. And then there's the taxi green, which is darker than the color of Netto's carrier bags, actually quite close to completely orange. Orange is the new black, they say. Or maybe it was a couple of seasons ago? You can't keep up with everything. Not all the time. But I think it's still true. Orange-colored as the prison suits in American prisons. Apparently a sign of the times.

But I'm listing for red. I'm on foot, and it's just past midnight. And there are no beetles or other traffic nearby. But basically you get fined if there's a patrol car. But why would there?

At the next intersection, there's red, too. I'm about to go over, but then I hear a siren sound a little away. So I'm going to stay and wait. Is it coming this way? The sound is still there. It's hard to determine the direction. The light is still red. It will remain for a very long time, I think. Finally, there's the siren sound there no more. But the light is still red in my direction.

Now I'm going to find out why. That's because there's such a silly little box with a button you have to press before it changes. I mean, in the pedestrian area. Even when it changes to green for the cars. I don't want to do that, so I'm just going to walk over without going and pressing any little weird buttons. Then I finally got over the traffic less traffic lights.

What a silly system. But the municipality probably has some explanation for what they themselves think sounds hugely convincing. They always have. Such a variety of the common good and the best sense, formulated in such a way that even small-minded officials can rave it off in their sleep without their bothering their newly cut heads and their shaved soul.

But something is happening. Even in public places, or perhaps just there, the last remaining pipe smokers must go outside in the waiting period until it is completely banned. But Dad himself is one of them, and he already began to complain about the difficult situation of the pipe smokers many years ago. And in the meantime, it's only gotten worse.

And then there are the cigarette packets with those scare pictures and warning texts. Jaeh, it's probably very good – if you're not a kiosk owner. But I know a guy who's starting to pick them up while there's still a bit of a scum in the design. He collects them, all the different flavors. Like others, they collect cards with footballers. He is working on getting a complete collection, with all the different flavors. All the different cigarette brands combined with all the different horror and warning images. He says some of them are more rare than others. Like if you collect football cards or something.

He thinks they'll be worth a lot of money one day when all the cigarette packets are made completely anonymous, so there can be no logo on or special design or anything like that. Especially if you have a complete collection. So it's an investment, he says.

Now that you don't get any interest if you put the money in the bank anyway. Then he has an excuse to keep smoking. You can always find a justification if you want to find something you can invest in, preferably with a very good reason. At least good enough to convince you that you're on the right track.

Otherwise, we risk being left on the platform when the train is running because we were sleeping over us, or forgot our travel card, alone and miserably abandoned. So we'd better hurry up a little bit to wake up so we can participate in the dream of the future of society, where we drive some kind of taxi in the morning, something uber-like something – they'll probably come back again, I think. At least until the driverless cars take over.

But until then, drive a little taxi in the morning, or at night maybe, and then go fishing in the afternoon (if there's still fish in the water) and maybe perform some stand-up in the evening – and then rent out the desk room or broom cupboard as a hotel room for to earn a little extra – if only we make sure to check the guests' identity card, so we are sure not to do anything wrong by renting out to someone without the right kind of residence permit.

That sounds a bit like what I once heard was supposed to be old Karl Marx's dream of communist society, that is, in a somewhat updated version. But I am even in the dream, this cheerful neoliberal semi-communist hippie manifesto about the digital supersociety, where all the great ideologies merge into one great ecological bulb ouster, which is nevertheless so mischievous that only those with a really great Think tank in the back can get a really rewarding and solid bottom line out of it, but so can they. Big time.

But for all of us, it will hopefully remain a beautifully illuminating and glittering dream, to which, of course, I also subscribe as long as it behaves in a civilised way. I'm going to continue to do that for as long as possible. Right up until the day the nightmare breaks loose and we are brutally awakened by the roar of the imploding virtual world.

But let's enjoy the dream as long as it keeps the beauty.

Chapter 9

Where I continue my walk, but now I'm not poetic anymore, for I get to thinking of the digital hippies, and Karl Marx and Lazy Robert. OMG!

So now I thought it was time to think a little deeper about things. Sometimes you get to do this when you go for a late-night walk or night. Whether you've planned it or not.

But let's forget about the IT bubble and the housing bubble and all the other bubbles that have been. Otherwise, you're just going to get in a bad mood. This time, it's going to be better. And who knows, maybe life just consists of a whole series of bubbles, one after the other, and then it's all about being fast enough and supple enough and ahead enough of it all, to rush off from the old bubble and skip over to the new one right in the right Moment. I think that's actually a pretty smart point of view to have. Very convenient and very appropriate. At least right now, in this bubble we're in at the moment.

If we're just open to it, there's probably golden times ahead when technology and the digital and the new advanced robots are doing all the hard work, so we can concentrate on having fun and relaxing and enjoying life. Maybe it's actually something you could call the Age of the Lazy Roberts,- or just lazy people in general - who is ready waiting for us there in the pipeline for the future.

I actually think this Lazy Robert guy would love to be such an Uber-style taxi driver who can drive a little taxi with his own old scoop when, incidentally, it fits into his other plans and when he's just in the mood for it and needs a little extra money. Kind of hippie-like, where he does that way and lets the desire drive the work and doesn't have to either apply for a permanent job or be sent into activation.

In fact, it sounds a lot more fun and laid back. Especially if you don't have one or fancy training with some great career opportunities that stand and flash ahead. And next door you can blog about something that interests you a lot, and score the checkout on it if you scratch it, so there will be some ad dollars.

Imagine if this is how we can all live in the digitalized future. That sounds considerably more fun than having to meet at a shift in a factory at shit in the morning and standing and working half-tainted for 7-8 hours every day. So I say absolutely blob hooray for the robots. Maybe lazy Robert has just been a little ahead of his time.

Now we're just waiting for that bubble to arrive for all of us more ordinary people, so that the golden times can begin. Meanwhile, the game continues on who should be allowed to join and who should be put outside the door.

And now, ladies and gentlemen, rien ne vas plus, as the croupier in the casino says when she sets the roulette in motion. And the wheel spins, on to the next chapters. This is where everyone gets to move on.

Well, that was pretty good, I think. She didn't think I could do anything like that, I believe! Okay, not so intellectual, but that's so boring. But this is probably the kind of thing that Mona's sister will love. The woman I made that bet with, she's doing a lot of social criticism and things like that. So I think it's for her.

Ha! I don't think she expected me to do that!

Chapter 10

Where I'm bored, so I think it's about time something exciting happened

It was at the café. It was a little thinly occupied. That's probably why I answered him, when this guy talked to me.

Everything's fake and nothing but fool's herring, he said. What is, I asked. Everything, he said. That was pretty inaccurate, but he was also well-varnished, I noticed.

The dark and stormy clouds of old are still hanging over me and tormenting me with their bursts of cold rain, he said.

Bullshit, I said.

I had a suspicion that he enjoyed reveling in that kind of thing. And at the same time he appealed to your pity in way that made me think of animal. It wasn't exactly my style.

He does it all the time. To everyone. I've seen him at the café before. It's the same every time. It's going to be a little monotonous. Now I had just fought my way out of my own self-pity, and then I had to sit and listen to his.

It can be quite hard. Just like when I stopped smoking, and everyone around me just kept going on. That's really hard. It becomes difficult to maintain your own smoking cessation. Or cigarette parking, as I call it, if it's a little temporary at first and you're not quite sure that it will last. Then you can always just park the cigarettes for the time being. One month at a time, for example. Sometimes that might be the way to do it. It worked for me, anyway.

But back to that guy who sat across from me. Now he started complaining about the weather. The world's most devoured subject. When he can't think of another sting or has been through the whole list, it's the weather that he's addressing. Now it's blowing too much. Now it's snowing, now it's cloudy. Now it's night frost. Now it's drought. Now it's raining all the time. Now it's blowing even more. Now it's too hot. Now it's too cold.

But I don't care. I don't give a pitch black hip-swinging damn about it. That's right. I just don't care about the weather. Unless I have to go out into harsh weather myself, of course.

Chapter 11

Where I get myself together and go home
to sleep. At least, that was the plan

Okay, I didn't want to sit there anymore and listen to that crooked guy. I thought I might as well go home. I needed to get some sleep, too. So I went outside and looked around a little bit while I thought of this and that. And now I'm going to go into the present sense, because there was this special mood that kind of grabbed me a little bit. When it's in the present sense, it seems like there's a little more pace, and that might be needed on such a lethargic night as this one.

So that's it. Those semi-dark streets, they call for something. I don't know exactly what. It's just such a touch of a vibe that grabs me as I walk under the bulging tree tops of the big trees. Suddenly I don't want to go the right way home. But just kind of random somewhere. Maybe it's some old memories knocking on the phone. Something that once mattered. And who still does it anyway, even if you don't think about it on a daily basis. I don't know. Maybe it's such a nostalgic thing. It could be. Some years ago, I spend a lot of time in this part of town.

The street is more or less empty. Rush hour is over. Almost no people on the sidewalk. Only a few cars on the street. A single cyclist rushes past on his way home. People are eating dinner now, here in the hour before it gets really dark. It won't be long before the lights are turned on and their gritty lights make it even darker in all places where there isn't just a lamp. Lights are already on in many windows. Some are ajar. Scents of many kinds of food mix here and there with the stench of a pot that is burned on.

I suddenly know that there is no point in looking for a shortcut behind the old workshop buildings that are in there on the right. And also not just going into the yard behind them, where the garbage cans stand and where there was once a passage way, so you could walk that way through. I'm going to know how long it's been, all that, past, it's no good. Never go back to a fuser. Even though this is where I met Anette. Silly, silly, that was so long ago. I think I'm getting sentimental. Move on. Just follow the ordinary regular sidewalk. Stay focused. Don't give in to the strangely seductive course of the old swine errands. So I'm going to hurry up.

Chapter 12

Where I had planned for something very exciting to happen, but as it turned out, it was just this guy in a laundromat struggling with a pizza. Sorry, but that's how it was that night.

Like I said, I was walking along the sidewalk with healthy steps. Not decidedly slow, in any case. Now I want to be a little more focused. So I continue the determined course along the gray tiles of the sidewalk.

In a laundromat, a man sits and patiently eats a pizza while his laundry runs around and around the machine. He's alone in the laundry, sitting all alone and eating his pizza. He awkwardly separates the triangular pizza pieces with his bare hands. Apparently the pizza man didn't cut to the bottom before slamming the lid on and handing him the box. Now the man sits and fumbles to separate the pieces.

I've tried that myself. It actually happens quite often if you buy your pizzas in a half-bad place where they don't make them properly. And where the bottom of the dough is also very often much too thick and there is far too little stuffing on top.

I can see how he is sitting there, struggling with it, several times the pizza pieces break in the middle when he gnaws at one of them and doesn't quickly enough stuff it into his mouth. Then some of it ends up on the floor, and then he kicks it under the bench that he sits on, in a very aggressive way. It's a mess. Maybe he's drunk since he's fumbling like that, or maybe he's just tired. Or maybe it's just because it's a pizza that's mega poorly made. I really feel with him, in such a little bout of empathy that suddenly comes over me. You can have that every once in a while.

But I have to move on and continue my restless journey through the night. Nonsense, it's not even night yet, it's still quite early in the evening. But it sounds like a little more something, when you say you're going wandering through the night. The evening, that's something else. So I continue on my way into the darkness between the scattered street lights. A piece of coloured paper flutters along the sidewalk, settles for a moment, then is blown up again by the next gust of wind, jumping a few feet further on its restless route through the empty streets of the city until sometime later, it might be cornered in a deserted parking lot or a run down, closed down gas station, where it can't move on. Sometimes I feel a bit like that myself.

Chapter 13

Where I Get A Little Embarrassed Over
Some Old Memories

I walk on, along the same sidewalk, down another
sidewalk, and yet another, and as I am walking along,
many funny and quirky thoughts pass through my
head. I remember one night, years ago, on a silly,
drunk and windy night, on the way home from a
party. I was only a young teenager back then. I made a
bet with another guy on which of two pieces of paper
first reached the end of the street. At the end there was
a bus waiting shed that used to be full of old torn
newspapers and ice paper and withered leaves that
had blown in there. We had written our names on the
pieces of paper so we could see whose that won the
race. Then we called up Katrine on my cell phone. We
knew she had left 5-10 minutes before us and was
waiting for the bus at that bus shed. And we told her
to keep an eye on it to see which paper came first. And
she thought it was totally silly, and it was, of course,
but she still said yes, she would watch out for them.

But then when we got there, both pieces of paper had been blown all the way into the corner under that little bench in the waiting shed, along with a lot of other stuff, so it was a hell of a mess to find them. I think it was after a school party. And said Katrine, Oh My God, I'm sorry. She forgot to keep an eye on that because she was talking to Bettina on the phone. And they both giggled quite a lot, and then of we got mad at her because she had promised, and she and her friend just thought we were totally stupid.

That's how silly we could be back then. A little embarrassing, but still I get to smile at the memory of it. I must have been very young. And fairly drunk, probably.

I move on, it's almost like my feet are just walking by themselves now. At the next corner, two crows feast on separate stale bread. With a suitable distance between them, isn't it just like many of us?

Chapter 14

Where I get home at last

I've reached a small square where there's a big tree. In the house facing the main square, there is a café, but it seems to be closed. The IS closed. Well and thoroughly, even. Looks like it's been a long time since they've been open. Maybe it's bankrupt or something.

But there's something about that house there on the corner. Something I'll have to remember sometime, I think. But not now. I don't even know exactly what it is. it must wait until another time. I'll stop for a moment, but only for a moment. Then I'll move on. I don't want to think about it now. I'm not in the mood. Just move on.

A cat swerves inside a backyard where the gate is open. Another cat, bigger and more disheveled, sneaks out of the next gate I come by. It looks hungry and peeled off. It runs and greedily throws itself over half a toasted sausage that lies and floats under a waste basket that is filled to the brim.

In walk quickly past the three small side streets with the low old houses, it is almost a kind of townhouse. I can't believe they're still there, but I don't want to think about them right now either. It's no use, no matter what, and it doesn't matter. This is where my father once lived, for a short period of time, after they divorced. Only a short period of time. And then what?

I'll keep moving on. Walk past shops that have definitely known better days. And also some that still seem to be pretty good going on, even a few of them I remember. And then there are the new ones that have come in. Which has moved into some of the old ones. A completely different kind of stores that look too new and different seem to fit into the context. But it's just because I think about it the way it was back then. I can't believe it wasn't long ago.

But it's not really about me. I just need to move on, I don't want to keep running around here all night. I follow the same street well before I finally turn down a side street and slow down a bit. The wind is sweeping in front of me. It's hardly raining. It's almost just some splashes that come with the wind. There's no reason to think I'm wet.

Now there are even fewer people on the streets. The few who are rush past, with raincoats on and with posted umbrellas waging a tough battle against the wind. But I don't do that thing with the fact that it's raining. It just drips a little from the lampposts and branches of the trees. It's nothing to talk about.

I'm speeding up again, my steps are fixed, I'm targeted. I'm going the route I'm going to take. It's time to go, whether it's raining or not. The route, the road that I set out at the time. I'm only going to find out now. Once, I walked it almost every day. But it was once in the past. Now it just has to goose down to get it done. That's what I've decided. And I'm sticking to that.

I continue on my path, intertwined and determined. I don't take care of the things I come by. I don't want to do that. There's no reason for that. It would be a waste of time and energy. I've already come too dad to turn around. It's just going to be finished, this. The tour just needs to be completed, completed, brought to an end. Once again, just for the sake of principle. I don't think there's anything else left.

I don't need any other reasons either. It would just make it more difficult. Keep it simple, sweetheart, I keep repeating to myself. Just get it done. And then get out of this maze of old hidden memories and what do I know. Just get home. Home and into the heat. Suddenly I'm completely soaked, walked off without outerwear, wet to the skin. Why am I only going to find out now?

Chapter 15

Where I decide to change tracks. And more than that, an evening with some of my friends sort of evolves

Now here comes something else. Something that happened recently. This is interesting.

But it was the other day when a few of my friends were at my house. Kenneth, Michael and Brian. The four of us. Such a little peaceful get-together. It started with us watching some football on TV. It wasn't a particularly exciting match. Not one of those that will to go down in history. That's when it happened. We got into a little special discussion. I don't really know how we just got there, but it doesn't matter.

It resulted in something Kenneth told me. It was something he'd read something about somewhere. And it wasn't even a joke. It was something about the declining number of children. The birth rate, which is falling all over Europe, threatens to shrink the population of the European countries. I think it would be very good for the environment and that thing with

CO2 and all that. No, I think that was enough in Germany, and not in the Netherlands. In such a rather large German city, or medium, at least. Not one of the big ones like Berlin or Hamburg. No, I don't remember what it was. It's so important, either.

But they obviously had become very preoccupied with the declining birth rate. So they discussed what they could do about it themselves, so to knock it up. Not just such an average family with a child and a half. Really get beat it up. But still in a fairly orderly way. Maybe a bit like when someone starts talking about the environment and the climate, and then there's always someone who says "Well, what do you do yourself to benefit the climate and the environment". It's not so popular if you're just complaining about something without even doing anything about it in your own daily life. So that's probably why they decided to make the kind of club like that to do something about it. In practice, that is. Don't just sit around and discuss it like politicians do. But do something about it itself, and then of course it had to be put in a bit of a firm framework.

What they envisioned was such a club of young men, maybe a whole 50-100 pieces, and should they make a promise that they would breed at least 50 children each. And then they had to make some statutes and some rules about the way it was going to happen when it was a club. And that was in Germany when they quite love having such rules and paragraphs and principles for things.

But it quickly became apparent that there were two factions in the group, so they should have just clarified that. I think there was a few that started out before they had determined how it was going to be done in such a way. But those breakouts, they were impatient to get started, so they just thought they could act it by some one-night stands with some random ladies when they went to the disco on weekends anyway. But they were quickly excreted as too superficial. It shouldn't just be such a random thing, the majority thought. There should be a little more system in it. And the men should have a relationship with the women. Maybe not a super-long relationship, but it shouldn't just be something like that with someone in a pub or disco that they'd just drunk drunk to get in their pants.

There should be at least one month's relationship with each of the women. There were even some who thought there should be two or three months relationship. But it was voted down because it would take dad too long if they were to make 50 children each. So a month was determined as the minimum. And preferably with a little infatuation over, or at least a serious summer flirtation, or something similar. Something that was also reciprocated by the women. A kind of serial honey-moons, as one of them called them, where you could go straight from one hot holiday flirt and honey-moon without everything else more troublesome in between. It had to be so cool and so hot, so the women themselves were keen to have a baby with them. But even so, quite noncommittal, as if it had been some young Greek god of a servant on a charter trip to one of the known – or perhaps more unknown – Greek tourist islands that had made them pregnant, and they were still madly in love with the guy. After all, women were not supposed to start demanding that they start to form a family and buy a house with the husband, because he had to move on to the next one. Someone immediately asked if the women would not be upset about being let down and abandoned in that way. However, the majority field that there is indeed a trend among many women today that they would like to be single mothers who do not also have a husband to take care of. There was actually a bit of debate about it, but they took a quick vote because there were many other things they should have discussed.

The main objective was, of course, to safeguard the population and to make an effort to ensure that the number of children did not fall too much, so that too few people were able to tackle the burden of the elderly when they once grew old. There was agreement on that. And then the other one had to go after it, so they were supposed to say a nice goodbye to the woman as soon as they were sure she had been pregnant. So they could get a lot of children out of it without having to spend too many years on it, but there was still some of the men who thought it was a little the women. So they suggested that one combine might it with creating a dating agency for what they called beta-males or beta-males, which would probably be much better suited to something like that than, who of course themselves perceived as alpha males. But that discussion was postponed until later because it was about to be late at night for that meeting they luck about it, and was covered up inside the restaurant next Door - with spit-roasted suckling pig and five different kinds of draught beer.

Chapter 16

Which is really just a continuation of Chapter 15, but something comes up about a secret initiation ritual. Wow!

But even during that party after the very inaugural meeting of that club, there were some who were quickly out and started to make some bets with each other about which of them could get the largest number of children out of it within the first year. But then it disagreed about the precise definition of it, it should be the number of children, or the number of pregnancies, that was the decisive factor. For what if there were some of them having twins, or maybe even triplets. Maybe even several times during the year. It wasljust something that Kenneth had read somewhere on the Internet, and which he was now trying to recount after his memory, even though he was a little unsure of some of the details. It was also quite late at night and both after the football match and a certain number of beers.

But now he went on and moved on to some of what he apparently thought was some of the really exciting thing. So we listened really well, because it sounded pretty colourful. It was something about those guys in that club, they'd done some kind of initiation ritual for the guys who were supposed to be in it. Or some test they had to pass before they started the project itself. Something like a pretty extreme bachelorette party, or something like that. Unfortunately, he didn't tell it completely coherently, because beer had to be drunk and chips eaten, and he was probably the one of us who had gone to the hardest during the football game.

But the rest of us pressed him a little to get him to tell us what that bachelorette-style ritual was all about, such in some concrete detail. I think it was something that was supposed to prepare them for the task, set them up for it, just like before an important football match, and at the same time test whether they could now also stand the distance when it came to it. I think there was something about some whores and some porn movies and some kind of manhood test, and then like the wildest bachelorette party, but it was a ploy to get him to clarify it a little more.

He was now pretty drunk and rummaging around a lot in the description. So Brian hit the table and demanded that he now tell us exactly how it was going, such point by point. After he had just sung a little, and we had given him one of the really good craft beers to strengthen himself, he actually started to get to the point and explain it in more detail. It began with, he said, that after some warm-up exercises that were special enough in themselves, all the men, one by one, and while the others watched, had to start proving that they really could.........

Here he got stuck because it suddenly rang the door. Several times and pretty powerfully. In the end, there was nothing to do but go out and shut up. That Kenneth was just starting to tell, so we could bring all the juicy details.

Chapter 17

Where Jehovah's Witnesses do not call, but then in turn is a cat going down from a tree, and Michael turns out to have special abilities

But they weren't Jehovah's Witnesses, nor any other of them. It was an elderly lady, on the other hand, who had called. I quickly recognized her as one of the neighbors and she was completely distraught that her cat had climbed into a tree and now couldn't get back down. There was nothing to do but go out and look at the case and see if we could help here.

We looked at each other. Who was most sober? Because there was enough doomed climbing on the ladder, or something like that. There couldn't be much doubt. It probably had to be Michael, because he had been spitting in the glass all evening because he was going to a big family party the next day, and then he didn't think he'd show up and be plagued by giant hangovers even before the first glass of red wine. Then his girlfriend would be massively angry, because it was her father who turned 70.

Michael was probably smart enough, so he quickly understood our joint decision. It wouldn't even have been necessary to say it out loud. He stood up with a sigh, because like the rest of us, he would rather have stayed seated and heard the story of that initiation ritual. But there was nothing to do, so he went out into the hallway and put on his windjacket. The rest of us followed so we could assist him if necessary.

It was inside the garden a few further houses along. The silly cat had climbed into a large tree with no special side branches at the underneath. And now it put up in the tree and couldn't figure out how to get back down.

It turned out that there was actually a ladder nearby. It hung very nicely on its decorated fittings on the wall of the old lady's garage. We dragged it to the tree and put it right on the tree trunk.

Michael started climbing up while a few of us stayed on the ladder. It wasn't that easy to get the cat. As well as climbing high, it also seemed rather terrified. I think it was a dog that had chased it up the tree, according to what the old lady explained.

But now Michael proved myself to have special talents. He started moaning like a cat. It almost sounded like it was something he had trained. It certainly sounded very convincing. I think it's almost like a female in maturity. It wasn't exactly pretty to list two. Once serious cat wailing.

The old man had already said something about the fact that it was a hankat. Otherwise, he might have chosen to mjave like a hankat instead if it had been a female, the old lady. Hatred. If he was so good at it, or it was just me who couldn't hear the difference. I'm not a cat expert.

But at least it worked on the cat up in the tree. It suddenly jumped into the arms of Michael, who was still standing on the ladder, and began to rub himself lovingly up at him. Fortunately, he managed to keep his balance there on the ladder, which we kept in a firm grip. But it was a bit of a task to climb down the ladder step by step with the suddenly very loving cat clinging to his clothes with a firm grip of its sharp claws.

But down he came and had the cat handed over to the old lady, who was exuberantly happy.

Chapter 18

Where we are hosted far above our ability
…..and go missing something else

The old lady, as I said, was so happy that we had her cat rescued from the tree. She insisted on showing her gratitude by inviting us all in for home bakes and a glass of sherry. We didn't think we'd be familiar with that. But one glass of sherry became more, while the sweet old lady began to tell about her three adult children, all of whom had done well in life, and went on to tell of all her eight supplemented by selected sections of her own life story. And continued and continued with it, while she generously kept welcoming the homemade cakes and opening a new bottle of sherry when the first one was emptied.

She lived alone in the house, and I think she was bored a little bit. The man had died a dozen years ago, which we also got a detailed account of. She was obviously happy to have some company. And she was also a little elated after the whole affair with the cat and her joy that she had managed to get the well-being down from the tree. Supplemented by the glasses of sherry she also set to life.

I must admit that both myself and the other three also took plenty for us by both sherry and home bake. Partly because there was little else to deal with while we politely listened to her long accounts, and sometimes tried to ask a question that sounded interested, even if it was not really necessary at all. And partly because had become both hungry and thirsty, after we had suddenly been dragged away from beer and chips and other kinds of goodies.

But even as it kept dragging on, much longer than we had anticipated, she was actually such a really sweet old lady, and full of gratitude that we had saved her cat. So we didn't want to disappoint here. Moreover, several of us were starting to get a little tired or downright sleepy, with the consequent lack of initiative to do anything else than just stay seated and let ourselves entertain. All meanwhile they quite a few glasses of sherry undoubtedly interfered with the very many beers we had consumed earlier in the evening, and in a way that was not completely simple to see through. It was in each not exactly the cocktail we had the most experience with.

In fact, it took a few hours for the seance to end, and we were able to leave the old lady's generous home bakes and generous accounts after she herself had started to sit and slit a little in between and had repeatedly declared that now it had been shown Soon, here bedtime, just for the moment after starting a new story about herself or her family with the introduction, "No, you should hear this too. It was then, then.........., and then it took at least ten minutes or 15 minutes before there was another chance to stand up and say thank you nicely for tonight – if we were otherwise fast enough. But finally, it seemed that she was serious.

Before we left, she thanked us once again for our efforts with the cat, before walking out to the garden gate. But then suddenly there was also a doomed break-up, not from here, but also from me. It was late. And no one was saying anything else than going to bed and sleeping, and we quickly said goodbye. It was a while before I saw any of them again, and then it was in a completely different context.

So I never got the explanation for that very colorful initiation ritual, and I still don't know how it went with those men's rather wild project. Were there any women at all who wanted to be part of it? And did the men really say to keep repeating 50 times when it was supposed to be done that way? Weren't there quite a few of them who burned really hot on one of those women, so they'd rather marry and start a family with her, and then drop the rest of the project?

When I got hurt once to mention that enterprise for Mona and her sister, they were both wildly outraged. So I quickly pretended it was just a joke I just made up and not something that seemed to have really happened in reality. I've tried to google it on the internet several times and try to find that website where Kenneth said he'd found it, but I can't remember what he said it was called. Maybe it hasn't been such a porn-like site at all, but something from a local newspaper in some small German town. I can't even remember what he said the city was called. But I'm still trying different keywords. Maybe one day you'll succeed.

Chapter 19

It is five weeks before Christmas and the windows are filled with rain

This isn't a very cool day. Or it's become night now, of course. Darkness has descended over the city. The wind is on. Night-time wind. Some metal junks somewhere outside. It's junking again. And again. A little break. Then it junks again. And again. Maybe it's an empty can that gets rolled back and forth on the street by the wind. The rain whips against the windows. The wind howls in a chimney. A branch strikes the house. Just like in a novel about a lonely and melancholy winter night. Or autumn night. The seasons aren't quite what they've been. It's the kind of thing that makes it hard to be a writer.

I get up and go to the kitchen to put coffee over. It's five weeks until Christmas and the windows are wet with rain.

I'll freeze a little while the coffee brews. There is also not proper heat on the appliances. I've had the caretaker several times, but it hasn't helped anything. As soon as the coffee is done, I'll pour myself a cup.

No, a mold. Not a cup, but a mug. It's about being precise. It's not just a mold. Any mold, I mean. It's one of those old grey stoneware mugs from that time. Shut up, there's a lot back then. Too much. But the hot coffee does well. I need that. I'm hungry, too. But I don't want to eat anything now. I should probably go to bed. Get some sleep. But I'm going to stay up anyway.

There's something about the night I like. Something honest, almost something naked. In self. Something sincere. Something no-nonsense. Something nitty-gritty. That's one of Monika's expressions. Well, not so much if you're rushing around town partying. That's not what I mean. Not right now. But a night like that. A little melancholy in the mood maybe. Suddenly, I still want to go out. Go somewhere. Where a little is happening. But I don't really want to. So I'm going to stay inside. Turns on TV. But there's not really anything interesting. I get tired of zapping around quickly. I'll have another cup of coffee. I'm going to butter myself a cheese. I'm going to eat it slowly. Chew carefully. It's slimy cheese. It doesn't taste like anything. I put half a slice of green pepper on it. But don't bother it anyway, and it's half there.

That's the letter I got from Monika the other day. But I don't want to think about that anymore now.

I don't really know what I'm going to do right now. Sometimes there's just nothing to tell, even if you're really trying to twist your brain to make it a little interesting. It's just a little thin and bland all and you've just run out of words worth mentioning without them hanging you out of your throat. That's just the way it is sometimes. Readers also benefit from being told this.

Chapter 20

Well, now I think that something very exciting is going to happen, or at least something else

Okay, now it finally looked like something exciting was going to happen. A Christmas party! Let's see what can come out of that or what actually came out of it on that special occasion. I'm just trying to write it down as best I can from what I remember.

But I just think it's a little bore, or a little wrong, rather, when Marlene says that there's plenty of everything, and there's not at all anyway. She does that all the time. That's the kind of habit she's got. She defines it in a very strange way. For example, she thinks that 4-5 beers in the fridge is enough. And it's not that there's no room. The closet is big enough, and it's never fully filled up anyway.

Marlene, she's the one I'm currently staying with, after the latest changes in my life. Yes, it's pretty new yet. Not so firmly. But almost. She says it's almost such a Christmas thing. But a little bit of everything can happen during such a good long Christmas break. At least for people with a slightly more colorful lifestyle.

It's probably a bit of a coincidence that it went the way it did. Maybe. One word took the other, and suddenly took off. That's the way it goes sometimes, and especially in this kind of hectic time leading up to Christmas, when it's all so upside down and you want to help the Christmas spirit a little along the way with both one and the other. Of course, it was at one of those pre-Christmas parties that it happened. Also called Christmas parties.

But it developed pretty wildly. At least in relation to what I had imagined when I was considering whether to agree to it. I had considered staying home. In fact, I had been to another Christmas party the day before and part of the night with and I was still a little affected by it. I thought about dropping number two and staying home and nurturing my hangovers and my pity with myself. But I didn't want to do that when it came down to it.

On the other hand, it is also conceivable that it was precisely because I had not mentally finished Christmas party number one, that I suddenly felt pretty wildly inspired to find my good old night will again and go to that no. 2 Christmas party too. It can't be ruled out at all.

I didn't really know Marlene beforehand, not much in any case. Only kind of more superficial. But when the Christmas party started, that is, the second one, I had no doubts at all. And in fact, she seemed really sweet and easy-going. That's true. So that's how it worked out. And as the evening unfolded, even more so.

Chapter 21

And there are two hefty women fighting over me right now!

We actually felt pretty good on the wavelength, or I certainly did. Maybe even more than Marlene. Or maybe I was just a little more vocal about it. But she's the one who invited me home. I would like to stress that.

It all seemed quite forgiveable, as far as possible in this genre, which I have been in for quite some time and which has probably almost passed me in the blood gradually. And of course, a lot of work here in December, when the blood is also often under the influence of other fluids, so it often goes into a higher unit, or even the opposite. But in fact, it wasn't just the Christmas month that was to blame, because I'd been along the way with something like that for a long time. After a fling with Charlotte, which didn't really come in the air anyway.

But I was really happy with the spoils. I mean, to have swapped between Charlotte and Marlene. Or to have been swapped between them, because I wonder if that was really more how it happened. Because when I say it as it was, it was not quite the case that Marlene was a kind of prey I had hunted down, like a hunter who goes hunting in the woods. No, it wasn't quite like that. I'm not as old-fashioned and oppressive as that. I'm not a male chauvinist pig! Actually, it was the other way around.

Of course, I have also heard the theory that in all the mammals, and therefore also in the most distinguished of them all, that is, the humans, it is the female who chooses her partner. Okay, you should just digest that. But then why not try to scratch it so you can get a little benefit out of it too. Because then it is also her responsibility if it turns out that she has chosen wrong so that it does not really work out anyway. It's not the poor guy's fault then. She's just the one who hasn't been good enough to choose. Ha, ha, smart note. At least I thought so.

But apart from December and all its being, it could actually look as if this time it was me who was the prey that was being abandoned. Or what was fought between Marlene and Charlotte. Sometimes it can be quite exciting with stuff like that. Sometimes. And maybe most of all when you are in a certain mood, trying too hard to repair your December damage.

Such a situation where most of it seems like a cheerful show, much better and more engaging than most TV series. And you'd be stupid if you weren't also a little flattered by it, especially if they're both cute and handsome and charming.

Well, it probably already crept a little between Charlotte and me when Marlene came into the picture. And as the Christmas party progressed and my night will awake more and more, it crept quite a lot, both between Charlotte and me, and between Charlotte and Marlene ….. and whatever. And then I don't want to mention anything about copy rooms. Where you make copies of everything from firing notes to declarations of love. I'm just fiercely opposed to most of what's being said in those kinds of places. That's it. Places like this are not meant to talk at all. Not beyond what is most necessary in any case.

But that's how it happened. Back then, I was too preoccupied with my Christmas spirit not to be very proud of it. It didn't come until later.

Chapter 22

Where the whole thing is going completely off the tracks and I think it is going to have some implications for where I'm going to live.

It turned out that there was some crunch in the supply of the dark green and brown beer bottles, which was a kind of foundation during the Christmas party. The problem, in short, was that Marlene had engaged in an alternative beer delivery, while Charlotte had been helping to arrange the important corner of the Christmas party, which was about the more official beer purchases. Here she, as a typical employee of an accounting department, had gone for the cheapest offer with a volume discount from some discount warehouse from a beer depot. It kind of says a little about her, too, doesn't it? So maybe it's no wonder I ended up at Marlene's. Not only did Charlotte know nothing about beer, she was also stingy, even with others' money.

Then Marlene would have shown much greater initiative and decisiveness. She had arranged for a rather nice selection of different craft beers, mainly foreign ones, both from Germany and Belgium and the Czech Republic and Spain and Mexico, and a few more places. There was really something to choose from, and all of super quality. She had done really well. And even though she had nothing to do with either the shopping department or the event itself, but just had a nice boss who let her do what she wanted. She even provided a very good selection of booze, which in a short space of time helped the party's attendees get out of the current reality straitjacket, as she herself calls it.

It's amazing that people can get into a fight about such things with beer and booze, for example on such an occasion like this one. I don't want to waste my time on that. I'm just drinking it, that's what it's meant to be. The problem, of course, was that, on her own initiative and bypassing the system, Marlene had provided some much better beer and a lot better booze than the officially purchased shim. Which, of course, was immediately denied by those who thought she had been a little too proactive and who stubbornly tried to perpetuate the impossible argument that one could not taste the difference anyway. Charlotte felt bypassed, and rightly so. She had probably already had some contradiction running with Marlene.

It seems a little obscure how it developed, and how far it went. But Charlotte immediately grabbed her part of the evening's disagreement and made a bit of a show out of it. We really managed to get it amber and get many more of the contestants carried away.

Chapter 23

Where there shouldn't be much to say about those Belgian trappist beers, but apparently there was.....

Even worse, it got much worse, or even more off the tracks, when someone discovered that some of Malene's beers had been brewed at one of those trappist breweries in Belgium, and immediately roared it all over the assembly. Which led a witty dog to roar back that he didn't have to talk out loud when it was just a brewery run by those trappist monks. That's how the mood had become at the time, and it even became moreso - when he threw himself with a longer explanation ofwhat it's all about with such a trappist brewery.

And that it has nothing at all to do with the fact that the beer was brewed that an old monastery from before the elevator was invented, although it actually is. But that's just not why it's called this, because it has nothing to do with stairs at all. Hay. But rather, it is about the fact that those who visit such a monastery can't learn anything about what it is about, except by listening to everything that is not said. Which, I think, is not quite true either, because I think it's only among themselves that the monks are not allowed to talk.

But of course there were some who had to embroider on it, now that the subject had been seen in exercise. Someone immediately pointed out the paradox that this trappist beer, which was traditionally brewed in deep silence, could make people as eloquent as this discussion was a clear example.

Then there was another one, and unfortunately I was the one who had become so eloquent of the fantastically good beer, that I aired a very profound theory at the time that this was exactly why. All the words that were not said in the monastery during the brewing of the beer, like still were hidden in the beer, as a kind of resource one could draw on, or rather got poured into when the drinking beer. Like if you put the money in the bank instead of spending it right away. And so in turn can use them later. What I saw myself was doing in rich measure. So those who saved words in the beer. I didn't even think my explanation was any trace silly until now afterwards.

Chapter 24

There's nothing to do about it, but here's something even more about those trappist beers and why they taste so good, but I refuse to believe that that explanation is right, it's probably just nonsense from a drunk person at a Christmas party. Or skip this chapter and move on to the next one, i might have gotten a little more sober so I don't think this kind of thing is funny at all. I'm fucking sitting here writing it down while I can still remember it, even though I should be sleeping it out.

But there was still a full time at that Christmas party. It pulled out, as does very often. And as is actually the intention.

They were still yelling and screaming at each other. I mean, Bodil and Malene, sometimes everything else.

They each had their own team of supporters who backed them, and now it was everything else they were arguing about. After all, they had already been through all the arguments several times, so it started to get a little monotonous. But then Bodil suddenly came back on the track with some more nonsense and began a long story about it to turn a little more sympathy onto his side.

The story went on that she had once heard of such a classic trappist brewery in the old days, when there was such a young monk who was a kind of apprentice who had to look to how it all went with that beer brewing so he could learn it himself. Who is a real professional brewer, took the lid off the large brewing kettle to load some hops and some malt into it. He's turned to take a sack of hops behind him. While he is fumbling to get a good grip on the bum, a large German shepherd comes running in through the door way out to the open open because of the summer heat. In front of the dog runs a poor cat, which the dog is hunting across the brewing hall. To get away from the dog, the cat takes a long leap over the open-ended brewing boiler, but it fails its jump and falls into the brewer's boiler instead, and drowns instantly.

Meanwhile, the dog drowns everything with its furious barking before running out of the brewing hall at the door at the opposite end, which is also open. The brewmaster, meanwhile, has a good roof on the bum behind and has loosened the cord that tied it together at the top. He just gets to see the dog as it's on its way out as he turns around towards the brewer's boiler again and starts pouring all the hops from the big sack into it. He clearly has no idea about the cat, which is located at the bottom of the brewer's boiler and is quickly completely covered in the hop.

The young apprentice monk does that in return. He's seen it all, but now he has a problem. He would, of course, like to make the brewmaster aware of the cat in the boiler. But because they're both trappist monks who have to live in silence, he can't say anything about it. Because then he'd violate the trappist rules. He is a pious monk who would like to do it all by the book, so he will not, of course, violate such a basic rule. And he's young and very keen to be perfect as a monk. So sometimes he interprets the rules extra squarely.

Instead, he tries to make some gestures with his hands to imitate a cat that comes running and jumps up into the brewer's boiler, but the brewmaster doesn't understand his strange gestures and just shakes the head of the silly kid. So he still doesn't notice about the cat.

The brewmaster just continues his work of pouring the other ingredients in, and then he sets the brewing process in progress exactly as he usually does. So that means that the poor dead cat is being brewed in the portion of beer that has just been started in the brewer's boiler.

Bodil smiled hoofing and looked a moment out over the congregation before continuing.

So can you see what I mean? She said. I just don't want to drink this kind of beer with dead cats in it. she exclaimed and the garbage laughed, so it was clear to everyone that she had at least taken plenty for herself of the other beer.

Apparently, she herself seemed to have demeaned Malene's fancy foreign craft beers, while providing a kind of justification for her own more drilling beer purchases, and that she had thus won the discussion about it with a kind of backhand fine.

She laughed at it herself, but it was nonsense. It was just a flat and stupid witty joke. It wasn't even really funny. She was funny at their expense. I mean, on the trappists. Those beer-brewing monks who couldn't even take a back on it without violating their own rules, as someone immediately mentioned. If they had been able to hear Bodil's nonsense, what fortunately they could not.

I bet that's not the case in real life. They certainly have some way of pointing something out of this without having to open their mouths to say anything about it. there should also be something on the label that it was not suitable for vegetarians, and I am not aware of that. It was simply below the low target. I tried to explain that to Bodil, too.

But she didn't want to give up, maybe that's exactly what's the manufacturing secret, she said. Maybe it's what's at the heart of their secret recipe that makes it so unique, she said, and cheered as she looked around for more applause, and the garbage laughed as the loose roof tiles at the neighboring house shook. Oddly enough, it made happiness with many who cheered and clapped as if she was the queen of the party and the story of the dead cats in the beer was one of the evening's highlights.

Chapter 25

The Christmas party is still going on, and its philosophical heights have probably reached a new low, for now there is a long talk about those trappist monks who are guaranteed not to have such a Christmas party like this.

Charlotte, of course, basked in the rush of enthusiasm. But soon got into gear when a middle-aged overbooker began to explain something about how he thought it went to such a place.

She was very dissatisfied with this, and therefore tried to retake the course by shouting outside the assembly if anyone knew if those trappist monks had to send text messages to each other.

But no one knew that, and he quickly took the floor again and went on to say that they probably don't use cell phones and computers in such a place, because it all happens after centuries-old methods and some special old ones. recipes with hundreds of years on the back, and that's probably why the beer gets that special aroma. It would not make sense at all if they had mobile phones, when they are not allowed to talk to each other, and even with text messages they can have long conversations with each other, so that would be pure cheating, he said.

But on the other hand, he continued his long and very loud lecture on it, so they have probably developed their own methods of dealing with such things as the one with the cat in full silence. They've been brewing that beer for centuries, so they've probably found a solution to it too. Maybe they have such an old mechanical apparatus sitting on the wall inside the brewing hall, like that back from the old days. One of those things where you just have to pull a act and then a metal sign is tilted up where it says. "Have you remembered to put yeast in?" or "Remember to use the right type of malt" and then of course one that says: "Beware! A cat has been put in the brewer's boiler!""

I think he thought it was funny. But not many others thought so. I didn't think so either. For once Bodil hit the nail on the head when she said it was both corn and nonsense and pure nonsense and also rather prejudiced. Most people actually applauded that, and in return, the accountant clapped in.

Those discussions went on around and distracted some others who were just as silly. But in the end, a little more calm fell all over the place, and for a while it all seemed pretty normal. Charlotte and Marlene didn't yell at each other quite so much, either. It could now be quite entertaining in between. But now, I think there were only a few small frictions left between them.

That's how I perceived it, anyway, because I'd become so sleepy from all the talk about beer, so I actually spontaneously took a little nap, well laid back on something that looked a bit like a couch. Luckily, Marlene woke me up before we went home. Maybe she thought it was a hassle if she had to drag me down the stairs.

Chapter 26

Where the gas goes quite a lot of the balloon, as it is often after a good Christmas party. But I think this is more serious like

Of course, I had Christmas with Marlene. It was actually very nice, but maybe something different than I expected. For example, I don't know why she invited Charlotte to our first Christmas Eve together. I mean, Charlotte. I thought they were tuxedo unfriended and really hated each other so much. But now they were chatting like old girlfriends who had known each other forever. And on the whole, it wasn't just the two of us. It was kind of weird. But I don't want to sit around and spread about it in every detail. We shouldn't just say that it's a matter of privacy, what more specifically happened that night.

Chapter 26

Where, frankly, it's not very funny anymore

Then it's the Christmas Day. And Marlene has left on Christmas vacation and she's not alone and I'm just sitting here having to come up with something so as not to get food. It's completely out of hand. That's not how I intended it.

Back then with Bettina, we used to call it 1st Christmas Night, 2nd Christmas Night and 3rd Christmas night. And we used to give each other gifts three nights in a row. But that was then. It's not like that anymore. Now here today I woke up late, even though I hadn't even slept very well.

There's not really anything to stand up to on such a 1. Christmas. Especially not when you're alone after a slightly strange Christmas Eve when it didn't quite go the way I wanted.

They've both left. Both Marlene and Charlotte. Home to the family in the province. Each family, each its own city. But they were following onto the train. They might as well, they said. It almost sounded like they had planned it in advance.

So now I'm just sitting here staring. I expected us to be together all Christmas, Malene and I. It's really sour show. I'm just sitting here getting really bored. What to do such a gray and sat 1. Christmas Day when you don't have anyone to do it with?

I had to come up with something. So after a little late breakfast and a little late lunch and a little extra care for my hangover, Then I decided that I go to the café where I usually come. Just to see if they happened to be open on such a high holiday.

In fact, they did. So I went and put down. There weren't very many people. But a little while later, a couple of the others, the ones I usually meet up with over here. They had the same problem and had the same idea. So we got together and got something properly put on the table. This hidden Christmas spirit had to be washed down with something.

The conversation got off to a slightly silly start. But what else can you expect on such a day?

It was Martin who laid out.

He said: I was out missionary my running feet just this morning, and in the square, the Salvation Army stood and used their message with full brass soup and everything.

I had to intervene.

Stop, stop, you said. You're using the words all wrong. It's called exercising its lion feet, not missionary, and the Salvation Army doesn't exercise in the square. They're missionary.

Martin: You're saying it wrong, too. I didn't say lion's feet, but running feet.

Now Paul mingled and said: 'There are a lot of words that say 'b' as 'v'. For example, the word copper.

Kenny wanted to be in, too: it's only if it's spelled with two B's. and running feet don't.

Paul Again: What about pepper. There's only one b.

Kenny: well, it's pronounced as if there are two b's. or rather two v's. Pevver, they say.

I just had to put it back back on track again.

Well, you said. They say 'I'm just a lion' with two v's instead of a single b.

Martin: Well, you're still saying it wrong. Then don't sit there and say lion-feet. Then you'll say leafy feet.

With two v's. Otherwise, you're breaking your own principles.

Kenny felt he needed to be smart again:

What nonsense. It's not that complicated at all. It's all connected. The difference is that when my boyfriend looks around on the sidewalks and exercises, she is so missionary for a healthy lifestyle. I can tell you that. She likes to admit that herself. And when the Salvation Army stops in the square and missions with speeches and songs and horn music, what are they doing? Yes, they are practicing to penetrate with their message. And practicing is the same as exercising, and exercising is the same as exercising. So it can be said that they are exercising their convictions to train their message to have a greater impact. It's very simple. It's all connected.

Finally, he finished his long smear, and now Paul had to say something.

It used to be two other words that you link to horn music, he said, laughing at the butter.

Martin: Damn not in the Salvation Army.

I just hate to correct.

Well, that's just a theory about what you've got there. But basically, you have no idea what they're talking about when they first start taking it a little more casually with the horns. You're just guessing. Or maybe you have prejudices about them? You don't have any concrete knowledge of it.

Paul: It's just as frivolous to accuse my girlfriend of everything. You're absolutely ridiculous if you think she'd lie down with someone from the Salvation Army.

I made a valiant attempt to recap before it ended up up all the way out in the hemp:

Well, when you exercise, you move your foliage-feet. The ones you Lions On. But when you're out to mission, it's important to stand firm on your good solid lion-feet, so that one is not overthrown by random reluctance or mistrust, or simply by a lack of responsiveness to the message you are coming up with.

It is that simple, I said, and added: and at the same time so complicated.

But it was mostly to make it sound a little deeper and more philosophical.

Paul raised his hand and made the V-sign with his fingers while he said:

Remember the V sign, friends! It's important! If we just remember our v's and the right number of them, then everything will be fine. Then we'll succeed in both the exercise and missionary work and everything else. As long as we don't shy away from the v's!

Martin: what nonsense heads though. Bowl!

And that was probably the most sensible thing that was said in that discussion. So I rushed to agree with him.

Chapter 27

Where we get much more serious .....
much more than I would have thought we
could under the conditions

This is going to be a whole diary. Second Christmas Day. Well, we met at the café again. Already at lunchtime. What else were we supposed to do? We even promised each other that it would not end in nonsense like yesterday. So the talk took a slightly different direction, we got to talk about those self-driving cars, which there's so much talk about. In some places at least. I think it was Martin who had seen something about it on TV. But he just doesn't really believe they're going to make it through. Most people would very much rather have their own car to drive around in, he began. And even run it. There's a lot of public transport over those self-driving cars. Too much city bus. A kind of mini-city bus. Okay, it may well be that it appeals to some of those who are used to driving a lot in a taxi. Or to those who don't have a car of their own. Young girls coming home from party in town, or old ladies who don't have a car of their own. Or people who are just too poor to have a car themselves. But most people like to drive. Not just to be transported, but to control the car yourself. Even sitting behind the wheel and being the one who decides how to drive. These types are so enthusiastic about the self-driving cars. Where's the driving pleasure? Most people would rather have their own where they have chosen for themselves what model it should be and what optional extras it should have. And so you can have your own things lying in the car and not have to drag them in and out of the car all the time. People care a lot about their cars. The planners completely forget that. What about the car as a status symbol?

The only people who will think it is a step forward, they are the ones who do not already have a car. Most others will then think it is a retrograde step to be forced into such a mini-version of public transport. That's what it's going to feel like. Sounds like such a real technocrat idea. Something like they could have come up with in old East Germany or something like that. There they would probably have seen it as a very rational solution, and in such an eastern bloc country before the fall of the wall, they could have easily pushed it over the heads of the people, even if the people were not interested in it. Will they do this with us, too? Force it through so that there are only self-driving cars on the roads and all other cars are banned? Otherwise, they'll never make it go through in earnest. And then don't own your own car. Then you have to settle for an automatic taxi that comes and picks one up. And where you probably have to book the trip in advance, and get ready and wait out by the road in all weathers. People will protest wildly and fervently against that. Have those planners even thought about that side of it? Or is it just the kind of idea they've been devising up an ivory tower without any contact with ordinary people and their relationship with cars?

Chapter 28

Where it's still 2. Christmas Day, and Martin continues his lecture on self-driving cars

It was a long smear, he came along there, but now Kenny took the floor and turned it in a slightly different direction.

No more self-steering his own vehicle, he said. No more deciding which way to drive. Once they've got it forced there, and there's only self-driving cars, the next thing it's going to be enough for all the traffic to be controlled from above, from a central traffic planning centre or something. That is where the real efficiency lies. If you control all the traffic, for example, if you are in control of the traffic, you can use the traffic. in Copenhagen, from central level, the capacity of the road network can be made much better. For example, one can use the following: avoid long traffic jams during rush hour. Maybe by sending some of the cars along a slightly different route, or by giving priority to rush hour to those who are on their way to work, or going home from work. And then decide that if a pensions are going to buy in, it must be either before or after rush hour. Just as there is a curfew on pensions cards for buses and S-trains.

So there will probably be an overall management of traffic flows. It can be used for many things. For example, also to avoid traffic jams if a lot of people are going to a football game or a concert or another big event. Or maybe a demonstration that the authorities do not like so much because they might fear that it will cause a lot of trouble. It can be used for many useful things, he said. For example, if it is now a known criminal, a burglar or something worse who gets into a self-driving car, then the police can monitor where he is going and if they suspect that he is on his way to do something criminal, then they can intervene and steer the car somewhere other than where he has booked a trip to. For example, they may be able to use the following: Steer the car to the nearest police station. It can, after all, be used to fend off terrorist acts, for example.

But now Martin had enough of all the positives that Kenny had said about it.

Soå you have to just hope, he said that they make those self-driving cars, so they're impossible to hack. Otherwise, it could be pure chaos. Can't you imagine how some young people are hacking their own self-driving cars with some unsuspecting passengers in, and then giving themselves to race with them because they've hacked the wireless connections to them and can therefore steer them around, exactly as they please, or what about the risk of cyberattacks. Where a hostile country hacks all the self-driving cars in a big city and puts traffic at a complete standstill. And can they even be completely protected from being hacked? Is it even technically possible?

Chapter 29

It's still Second Christmas Day and what about the motorcycles, must they also be self-propelled. Paul insisted that it should be included as an independent chapter

Then it was Paul's turn. But it was something a little different that he had on his mind. It's because he's got a brother named Raymond who loves riding a motorcycle. And if all the cars are going to be self-driving now, what about the motorcycles? Should they also be self-driving, he asked. Then there won't be much to ride a motorcycle anymore, he added. But he was a little worried that that's probably how it goes anyway. So it's those technocrats and planners who really decide. That's how it usually wears off, he said with a slightly gloomy mine. The rest of us got him right, maybe they want to abolish motorcycles altogether? And what about mopeds? Will self-driving cars be the only mode of transport permitted, except if you walk or cycle?

We sat around and talked about it, and then the idea came up. An idea of what we can do here in these lukewarm days between Christmas and New Year. And then we had to discuss all the kinds of things that characterise development. We had suddenly become ambitious. We wanted to show that we could be serious if that's what we wanted.

So don't come here and say that but can't be serious in the days between Christmas and New Year. Okay, that was probably the most, because we were all alone in this time, and we were bored. Then we had to come up with something we could make time come with, here in these weird days. And maybe there was something we wanted to prove.

Chapter 30

Where it's still Second Christmas Day, there is one of us who also criticises the electric cars and makes an unrealistic proposal, which he absolutely wants to include

After a few pizzas and little else to eat and a few more beers and a coffee with a little more loose talk, we got together and carried on with the serious stuff. It was still 2. On Christmas Day, and shut up, we'd get serious.

It was still those self-driving cars that we obviously hadn't finished. Because it is also something about the fact that it should be electric cars. I think all cars should be so, according to what the politicians think. Although still very few of them are out on the roads.

Kenny was there right away.

He quoted someone who had said it would be mega-expensive. That it's going to cost the state a lot of money in lost car taxes. Because it will be necessary to eliminate the registration tax on those electric cars to get people to buy them, that was Kenny's first criticism. Perhaps more environmental improvement could be achieved in some other areas for the same money, he said.

But that wasn't the only thing. On the whole, he didn't particularly like electric cars. He thinks there's a lot of problems with them and that it might be a bit of a dead end. Or a waste of energy.

First. It sounds fine if the power to them can come from wind power. But i guess there's not yet. I suppose we have only reached that point once the whole of the country's other energy supply has been converted into renewable energy.

Next. He believed that it would be very expensive to build all the charging stations needed for electric cars. And yet there would still be problems with the short range of electric cars compared to petrol or diesel cars. The problem is that it takes so long to recharge the batteries. But if you abolish all private cars and replace them with self-driving common taxis, then of course that is another matter.

His third criticism is all the chemicals that are in the batteries of electric cars and the problems it can cause when they are to be scrapped.

We wondered why he was so critical of electric cars when all the experts otherwise regard them as the great thing. Was it because he had something else in his back? Yes, that's it. Typical Kenny.

His cockhorse turned out to be cars running on compressed air. Compressed air? We asked wondering. Yes, compressed air, he said. Cars where the pistons in the engine are powered by compressed air, and not by petrol or diesel. We asked him to explain in more detail.

Yes, it's actually very simple, he began. A regular car engine can easily easily be converted to run on compressed air instead. It doesn't pollute. It's just regular air coming out of the exhaust. And it's easy and fixed to refuel. Like with gasoline or diesel. Much faster than having to charge an electric car.

I didn't think I'd heard of that before. But yes, that's right. In fact, there is a company in France that has built a prototype for a car that is designed to run on compressed air. Moreover, the principle is not new at all, he explained. In the old days there were some small boats to sail around on the lake inside Tivoli. It was powered by an engine that ran on compressed air. I think it was an old Danish inventor called Ellehammer who designed them.

I was starting to get a little bored out this afternoon. Shut up, it's just Christmas and everything's quiet.

I've stopped showing what I'm writing about it to the others in the group, because otherwise they'll just come up with so many changes and additions they want to keep up with, and I don't want to.

What I wrote, I wrote. Sentence.

Otherwise, it's going to be too much trouble.

Chapter 31

Believe it or not, it's still Second Christmas Day, and we are still improbably serious. Now we've come to something with a flip button on the computers instead of that old-fashioned mouse from 1900-and-white cabbage that we're still fating with, so we get mouse arm and carpal tunnel syndrome

Now it was time to have a little more to eat and drink. We ordered a load of the café's best sandwiches and some slightly semi-expensive beers. It's only Christmas once a year. And by the way, it was Martin who was supposed to give this game.

We only had just finished swallowing the food when Martin was there again, that is, with a new topic of discussion. A concrete proposal, it was actually. But now we had finally moved on to something other than all this about cars. Now it was about computers. It turned out he had been a long walk around the internet last night. And he had grown so tired of sitting and scribble up and down on those different sides with the mouse and those scrolling shafts. So he had come up with a much better way.

He wanted there to be a flip button on the keyboard. That's what he called it. A flip button. So when you press it, it switches to the next screen. So you can browse through the content on a website, just like when you browse a book. Instead of having to sit and grease with the mouse all the time. Or on that pressure-sensitive plate on the laptops. It would be much easier and faster, he said. Then you don't get the mouse arm from having to sit and fencing with that mouse and hit it exactly with it in a very small field.

But then it had to be built up in a different way, i.e. the various sites on the Internet, Paul pointed out. Yes, of course, Martin said, then it should be divided into screenshots. That just matched what can be displayed on the screen at once, without having to fumble with the mouse. Like the pages of a book. But there may well be a topic that goes over multiple screens, like a chapter that fills many pages in a book. Then all the screenshots had to be numbered with page numbers, and that the front there should be a table of contents with the page numbers on each section. Then it would be much easier to find what you are looking for, instead of having to find your way through that branch or tree structure, where you often have to sit and guess below what subtopic it is, among other things on some of the public websites. The tree structure where it branches from above is such a real engineering thing that probably seems logical to those who construct it and know all the contents in advance. It's just not very practical for the ordinary people who need it.

But now he already made an addition. In fact, there should probably be three flip buttons. And they should be on the keyboard. One flip button must flip a page forward, the other must flip a page backwards, and the third must be one, typing the page number onto the numeric keypad and pressing flip button no. 3, and pling, then you get to the side right away. It would be much easier and faster than the current system, he said. He sounded really excited about his idea.

Chapter 32

I can't help it, but it's still Second Christmas Day and Martin is just moving on with his cockerels, and now I'm about to have some change.

Martin then continued in the same sheds. He has several stick horses in terms of computers and the way they are made. And now, apparently, we should have them all served. He believes that there are several things about such a laptop or a PC that are stuck too much in the past. Partly the mouse thing. And why do you still use the old-fashioned qwerty keyboard like on a 19th-century typewriter? And why is the screen on a laptop still in cross format, just like on an old-fashioned TV set. It would often be smarter if the screen was in high format, like most books. There is a real need for some rethinking, he said.

Paul was there immediately and said: and then you will go back to an even older technology, namely a book. A really ancient way of doing it. Why do you want to imitate a book?

Because it's more practical, he replied. On these points. But it's not just that, I want to update it to the present, instead of them being the same as when they invented those things, such as the computer mouse. That was 50 years ago. Back then, it's probably been very smart, but now we need a smarter way of doing it. The mouse is probably good at some things. But it's not very good if you're mostly surfing the web.

Paul again: but a smartphone, it's in high format, which you would so much like.

Martin: yes, but it's a rub. Why don't they make them so they're two-piece? Like two pages in a book. Two pages with different functions when needed, so you can have a picture on the left side and some menu stuff or the different functions on the right side. For example. Depending on what's needed. Then the keyboard could also get a little bigger. Or there could be a picture on the left and some text on the right. Or maybe a large image that goes over both screens if it's a cross-format image. Then make it so it's to close together in the middle, like a book. So it doesn't take up more space than the present one when you pat it. Then it's better protected, too.

Okay, then he'd have had a couple of his cockerels reacting while we'd patiently listened. But now we weren't talking about any more that day either. It was just combing over. The rest of the evening went with a little more to eat and drink, and a little plain small talk about everything else. So it even worked out. Now it was Christmas and for lack of better.

Chapter 33

Then it was the day after Second Christmas Day, and now I'm the one who's got something done about self-sailing containers that sail in bunches and even go up ashore.

Home and sleep well and thorough. Get up late, lazy a little to a start. But just over dinner, like that at one-time, we were ready again, at our café. It's actually pretty well done, I think. All four had turned up, this time it was my turn. We had to take a little change of heart, we had agreed.

So what I'd come up with was something like the self-driving cars. I suppose that principle could also be used in other areas. For example, that sea. I mean, some kind of self-sailing ship. So not such large cargo ships or passenger ships. That's not what I was thinking. It is about the container transport of the future. It is the individual containers that must be self-sailing. Then they can sail in unison and be steered from above, so to speak. Maybe from a helicopter hovering above the waters and sending them electronic instructions on course and speed and so on.

But at the same time it must also be a kind of ambifious vehicles with wheels underneath. So when they get to their destination, they shouldn't be hoisted to the quayside by a large crane. Instead, they just drive up a shore along an oblique sleamine, and then they drive on to the road and to where they are to be delivered. Just like regular self-driving trucks.

The containers must of course be coated with solar cells that produce part of the energy to propel them forward. Maybe some kind of rotor or advanced kind of sail that can also supply part of the energy. So they are at least partly driven by renewable energy. To least out to sea. Maybe they should also have some kind of wings, such some inflatable some in the style of those on a hung glider, just much bigger. Then the wings can carry part of the weight, maybe half, so less energy is needed for sailing. At the same time, there will be a really large surface to mount solar cells on those wings. The wings must be inflatable so that they can be folded up when the container reaches the port of destination and is about to travel on to the country roads.

So many were the words. The others looked a little wondering at me. I don't think they'd heard of anything like that before. They had little doubt about whether it could be done. But there wasn't much real debate about it.

Chapter 34

Where we continue on the same track, but today it is something about the railways, which I think is quite boring, so for my sake you have to skip it

Now we had reached the 28th. We all showed up at the café in the early afternoon. Maybe we were actually getting a little bitten by it, or we just didn't really want to think of anything else. Personally, I might also have a few extra reasons for that. Sometimes she gets a little nervous about whether she'll say I haven't written it quite so well. That there is a lack of context in some places, for example. There are probably some holes in between. I haven't had it written on it quite as often as I intended. There's been so much else. And I didn't plan it very carefully. It is often a question of such a more spontaneous impulse. And she's an academic, so she probably thinks there needs to be more order and structure and planning in things, and maybe I'll probably disappoint here a little bit. Some of the opinions people have said are probably not exactly what she thinks. Or what I mean, not least. It's just such a feeling. I don't know how she's going to judge it.

But I certainly know that she's pretty crazy about something like that with social debate. And also something like that with new smart technology and all that digital stuff. She really believes in digitization. That it will provide a better society, and all that. Maybe a better world, actually. She's a psychologist or a sociologist, I think. So it must just be something for here, what we've been sitting here discussing in the days after Christmas. Although she probably thinks we're a little tough on the self-driving cars.

Well, now I'd better get to the point soon. Today, Kenny brought an idea. Now it was about the operation of the train, that is, the railways. It was not a particularly exciting topic to face up to, I think.

Well, he thought it crazy that so much money is being spent on modernising train services. Now that it's austerity. On the whole, he thought it was a huge waste of energy that you want to constantly replace means of transport with some others that are a little smarter. Both with the cars and with the trains. First, all petrol and diesel cars need to be replaced by electric cars and a lot of recharging points and what do I know. Why can't people just let them up at home with themselves, he asked.

Then they could have a small wind mill in the backyard that supplied the power to their electric car. Perhaps not exactly the traditional type that has been criticized for both making noise and providing annoying light reflexes. But maybe rather a barrel-shaped wind rotor, for example. It should at least be the case that the wings are relatively short and sit on an axle that can be camped at both ends, because then it is much easier to get them to drive silently or very quietly. And if you paint them with a matte dark green paint, instead of the wings being glossy and white, then there will be no light reflexes either.

That way they could get a large part of the power for free because they produced it themselves, and then of course supplement up with power from the mains when it is not blowing. And that could be the saving of having an electric car instead of a petrol or diesel car. In return, the state could save all the billions it would cost if they were to exempt electric cars from registration tax. Okay, then the state gets a little less into electricity taxes, but it is not the whole electricity price that is taxes to the state. On the other hand, society will be able to save part of all the billions it will cost to develop electricity production sufficiently if all cars are to be electric cars.

Come on, he sounded like he had invented both the deep plate and the stones displayed and the solution to it all. He even said that he had written a book about it, which he was constantly referring to. But sometimes it can seem a little overwhelming when people come up with such a patent solution. Kenny Ruthabarga, patent inventor of the extra-deep soup bowl. That's what he should say on his business card. If he had one. But I doesn't think he has. He's not going to stop again once he starts talking about all this.

Now we needed a beer to wash it down with.

Chapter 35

Where we are finally approaching the railway trains, and it is not very hard to control at all, as long as we just sit here and talk about it. But that's not the only thing we're talking about.

It was Kenny who continued. That is the thing about the fact that first petrol and diesel cars must be replaced by electric cars. In other words, some of the ordinary people in whom people sit behind the wheel, and then in a few years' time they will have to be scrapped and replaced with self-driving cars, which may also be a little bigger and more spacious, a kind of minibus , maybe. Or something like that, except that it seems most are pick-up trucks that run on diesel. But as far as size is concerned.

And then he asked if it's not a huge waste of resources. To have such a short intermediate period, during which all cars will be replaced by individual electric cars, which will then be scrapped and replaced by self-driving cars in a few years' time. So why not pat the horse and wait a little longer with it so that you could merge the two shifts and go straight from the current cars to the self-driving electric cars. It had to be more rational, he said.

But now Paul wanted to get involved, he said the self-driving cars probably didn't last very long either. No, the future was passenger drones, he said. After all, they were already being seriously experimented with in one of those super-rich little Gulf Arab states. So I'm sure that would be the future here too, he said. So why not skip two intermediates, both individual electric cars and the driverless electric cars, and go straight to the passenger transport of the future. Of course, the passenger drones should also be driverless or self-flying, i.e. steered from a central location, so that they avoided bumping into each other. And then they had to be equipped with some wings a la glider, which carried most of the weight, so they didn't use nearly as much energy. And with solar cells on those wings. But of course also with some batteries so they could fly in the evening and at night. I couldn't quite tell if he said it the most to provoke or if he was serious.

But the rest of us didn't think that sounded very serious. In fact, all three of us were prepared to bet that there would be three waves of new means of transport. At least. Probably even more. Even if they might come in quick succession. I don't think there was anything to do about that. Then you just had to find some other ways to do something extra for the climate and the environment.

But now he was addressing his next issue. It was train service. There, he also believed that there was a risk of a large waste of resources in the case of costly misinvestments. Why was it so important that you could get 20 minutes faster from Copenhagen to Aarhus or vice versa. It cost billions. Imagine if you had spent that money on reducing the ticket price instead. And now there was talk of electrifying the long-distance trains. I mean, those who drive out in the countryside. But surely this is not the one that is most needed to reduce diesel emissions. And again, it costs many billions, he said. I wonder if you could get more value for money in some other places. He was really outraged to list.

Chapter 36

Where there's even more to come about that train operation

But it wasn't even the worst. Because weren't the old-fashioned railways already obsolete? The future lay in those superfast trains that Elon Musk is experimenting with, with the Tesla cars. That brand new rail system, there's a kind of giant pipe post. Where some closed train carriages are sucked through some huge tubes using vacuum, and therefore can run much faster than old-fashioned trains. And even uses much less energy. That is what is the future of modern train operation, he said. Why not go ahead with the existing trains for a few more years, and then move straight on to replace them with the type of Elon Musk-type trains. Instead of spending many billions to electrify the current old-fashioned railways, in a surely quite short period of time. Or lock us in for years on a technology that will be obsolete in a few years' time. But that has been so costly that you have to go ahead with it for many years to come. Is it just symbolism, he asked. The kind of thing that you want to show your good will towards the environment and public transport, and the ultimate symbol of it, has become that you want to spend a lot of billions on it. , in terms of pollution or passenger numbers.

Apparently it was something that could really excite him. But Paul didn't agree at all. Those Elon Musk probably a few years in the future. And they would probably be far too expensive, too. The replacement of the current rail trains would have to come from elsewhere, he said. Because that's where he agreed with Kenny. But Paul believed that the self-driving driverless cars had to be able to replace both cars and trains if it was really approached. And then they could drive off in unison instead of rail trains, either on rails or rubber wheels, as long as a special lane was reserved for them and there were bridges or viaducts at all road crossings.

Linking them together could also be used when driving commonly on the roads, he suggested. For example, on the major approaches during rush hour. When a whole lot of commuters from Funen or South Zealand or Lolland-Falster were to drive the same way along the motorway towards Copenhagen, there was no reason for them to drive as individual cars with distance between them when they were still driverless. Then they take up dad too much space on the roads and give them long queues that we know only too well. It would be much smarter if an 8-10 pieces of them were connected to something in length with a bus.

Then you could make much better use of the space on the roads and avoid Queuing. When they were to be driverless and self-propelled, it wouldn't matter if they drove individually or if they were coupled a few. I believe that there was a Danish inventor who had already referred to this many years ago. So not that they should be self-driving, but that the cars had to be made so that they could be connected and run as a kind of train over long distances to save energy. Palle R. Jensen, I think his name was. And the system he had designed, he called for RUF transport. It was a case of having to build an experimental facility in Brazil or Argentina, where there was more interest in it than at home.

Come on, he'd got into the cases. I have no idea. It actually sounded like a very good idea. Especially when the cars were supposed to be self-driving anyway. The self-control thing was probably on the way out in a few years anyway.

Chapter 37

Where we continue after a little break, and now someone proposes something to encourage people to eat more vegetables and less meat

It was Martin who also had brought with him an idea today. But it went on something completely different. It was about the thing about getting people to eat less meat and more vegetables. That is why he wanted a tax to be imposed on all meat products. The money that came in would then be used to give all citizens of the country a kind of citizen's wage, which could perhaps be 100 dollars per month, depending on how much the meat tax was raised. But this special citizen's salary was not to be paid in money at all. It was to be paid in vegetables. Fruit and veg. For example, know that everyone got a special debit card that can be used to buy fruit and vegetables for in stores – and only that. This means that everyone can get free fruit and vegetables and plant dads in supermarkets and greengrocers for them 3-400 kroner a month. Because they pay with that citizen's wage card, so the shops don't lose anything on it. So Martin meant.

So now we'd be hungry. I don't know if it was to make up for all the talk and vegetables, but we all chose a big dirty burger for our dinner. Martin, too. But I don't think they had any dishes with plant dads on the menu, either with burgers or anything else. But, of course, he could have been content with a bowl of lettuce. I didn't do that myself, I thought I needed something more solid. But just for the sake of Mona's sister, so she's not entirely wrong about me, I'll just mention that I didn't care about that Burger. I got both a large tray of French fries and a medium bowl of lettuce with both tomatoes and cucumber slices next door. So I think there were almost more vegetables than meat if, for example, you had weighed it. Because I'm not at all.

Chapter 38

Where they also want to abolish the money - and income tax. Kenny even has a suggestion on how. Very specific

Now it was the next day. And all four of us turned up at the café again, about one-time in the afternoon. I wonder what we should be discussing. We'd been all around soon, I thought. But I was still surprised when I heard what Paul was doing.

It was something about abolishing the cash. This has been the first time that the general debate has been advanced. But he was very much in favor of that. Not so much for the sake of the shopping, he said, but to fight crime. If there were no cash, many different forms of crime would become impossible, or at least much more difficult. First of all, drug trafficking. Imagine if you could end the drug trade, he said. And undeclared work. And prostitution and the trade in heeled goods.

That sounded amazing. But there were immediate objections. Especially from Martin. He said that okay, we can decide to abolish cash in this country, i.e.

Danish coins and banknotes. But will people then not just start paying with Euro banknotes instead if they are doing something illegal. And then we're just as far away. In the case of undeclared work or goods or prostitution. People won't just use Euro instead, he said. Also with drug dealing. Or maybe it all will just move over to the web where people then pay with those bitcoins or other cryptocurrencies.

And then that proposal was like shot down.

But now Kenny came on to the field. He also brought a proposal from home. And now we really pointed our ears. He recently started talking about abolishing income tax. He even had a very specific proposal on how it could be done.

We could immediately hear that it has been one of his favourite topics, which he has probably set and thought a lot about. He started by saying that income tax was an old-fashioned and completely outdated system that belonged at the time in the industrial society. It belonged to the society that emerged from the first industrial revolution, he said. The steam engine and the labour movement a few hundred years ago. But now we were well on the start of the fourth industrial revolution, as digitisation is often called. Where things are done in a completely different way.

And where the values of society are created in a completely different way.

So a whole new tax system is needed that is much more up-to-date, he said. In a few years, the robots will have taken over many jobs and it no longer makes sense to Use the income from wage or other employment as a basis for state and local government income.

And now he started to become quite political. Because he mentioned that old Marxist concept of added value. As I think, there is something about employers taking part of the value that workers create through their work, rather than paying it all to the workers. Or at least give them a bigger share of that added value. And you know what's pretty funny?" he asked. Those people from the Liberal Alliance and the others who want more and bigger tax breaks, they actually have an argument that is quite parallel to the one that workers then used towards employers. But for them, it is just public spending that is the new added value that they think should accrue to themselves more. Just like the workers 100 years ago, they believe that they should themselves be allowed to keep a greater proportion of the money their work generates. Now it's just the treasure they're focused on.

But, he continued, the whole shift to a digital society of robots and automation and resulting high unemployment will in a few years create the need for new mechanisms to redistribute the money earned by the big digital companies, but not in a few years' time. a large proportion of the population must live in deep poverty. And it doesn't get any easier by the fact that most of the giant companies are located abroad. And I don't think some of them like paying taxes. Why isn't that what the left is busy discussing, rather than the most correct climate and other behavior, he asked. Do you not even have any economists left for longer who could do some economic analysis and develop some serious and thorough ideas on how to solve that problem? So not just some declarations of intent, but some concrete and well-worked proposals. He thought that was the most important thing for them to address. And translate into some practical policy. They are discussing much the same as the last fifty years, adding a little extra value policy and climate awareness, he said.

And that's how he went on for a while yet. He really gifted them the smooth layer. I was gradually getting tired of noticing it all down. In almost field more like a referent from a debate meeting of the local electorate than as a literary writer. It was getting a little sluggish. But now I had started it, and i suppose we had all the issues. It wasn't that long until the New Year, either. It was just meant to be something we could pass the time with here between Christmas and New Year. And now it was almost politics. And besides, it was getting late, but he just kept going on and on.

And he went on to argue for his big cockerel. In reality, there was not much new in it, and there was a great deal of prescriptive suggestion he made about how it should happen, so I didn't want to refer to that, because it sounds completely utopian. He'll never get the politicians on that. It will require too much change to a whole lot of things. This is completely unrealistic. Even if it sounds rather interesting. It's certainly a suggestion I haven't heard before, and superficially, it might sound specious, almost like a Columbus' egg. It's just too radical. So it is completely unrealistic that it can be implemented. There is dad too much inertia in the system for that. Then he can give up.

He even says he's written an article about it, or i think it's a book. And also about some other things. Something political. I think it's called something like "The Triple Division of the Economy," I think. That sounds pretty boring. I think he's pretty crazy about writing books about his cockerels. He's also the one who's written that book about people having wind mills in their backyard so they can charge their electric cars themselves, and all that sort of stuff. He's been really busy.

But we have overcome all that in these few days. It's become a lot more extensive than I thought. And now I want to go home to bed.

Chapter 39

Believe it or not, but all four of us are back up, albeit a little late. I wonder what we're going to be discussing today.

It had already been the next day and I had turned up again. Number two. The last two came down bit by bit. Martin didn't come until 3:00. We didn't want to get started until we were all here, but then we had time for a little late lunch and a few extra laps of drinking and a little no-nonsense small talk. It didn't seem like there was so much energy on today.

But finally he showed up, and then we had to get on with it a little more seriously. It started with us talking about some of the big hacker cases that have been. But it just turned into some loose talk, nothing very specific. I think we were getting a little tired of this concept now, too. We talked back and forth about all these problems and agreed that we certainly didn't know what to do with it.

We were already breaking up and going home when Mona's sister suddenly showed up. It turns out she's also written a book. Yes, she's used to that, something sociologist or social scientist, she calls herself, at a university, or a research site of that kind. That's what they call it, even if they're just thinking about how they think society works and how they think it's probably going to develop in a few years. That's the kind of book Mona's sister has written, and I think it's a little strange thing she writes. Is this really how she expects it to be here in Denmark in 15 years? That doesn't sound very nice. Several of things are a little far-fetched. I've only just been browsing it a little bit, because she didn't stay that long, and she brought it back when she left. It's called something like that far and high brow thing." 5 parameters for social development in Denmark during the Fourth Industrial Revolution around 2035". It was a hugely long title. Really academic. But that's what it's called.

But some of it is pretty creepy reading, I think. Although there is also some of what sounds to be a little more okay. That's the way it is. I only just had a look at it briefly. But it seems like there are both something positive and negative. Something where it gets better, and something else where it gets worse. I thought, as a rule, that books like the future were either about it going much better, or it went to hell. Either an ideal society or the opposite. But this looks more like a bag of mixed sweets. She would not answer whether she herself thought it would get better or worse in the future, in general. It varies from area to area, she said. In some areas it goes forward, in others it goes back – based on how we are used to perceived it today, she added. You didn't get much smarter from that.

She's been reading some of what I've written, kind of in portions, some chapters at a time. It was also part of that bet. So You had two. But she didn't sound so excited. Although she didn't really comment on it, but maybe I can catch up on some of this in the final sprint. I don't just want to lose the bet for that reason.

She was also pretty upset that I only refer to her as Mona's sister. But that's probably because I remember what Mona's name is better, because Mona herself is very sweet and okay. And her sister, well, I guess she's okay too, in her own way. If it's going to be that way. But her name is Louise Jorgensen. Then I mentioned it, and then it should be in place. Then no one can complain about it, nor any of the readers.

The others in the group were also there when she suddenly came in and got into our café. No, okay, she was just interested to hear what we had been talking about in those days between Christmas and New Year and hear a little about our views on the future. But she also wanted to talk about her own book.

Chapter 40

Where I'm going to tell you a little about Mona's sister's book, even though I had intended not to. But I'll make it short.

It was mostly three topics she mentioned. The first was that there will be much more individuality, because all that digital hardware and software make it possible. Private health insurance, private insurance against unemployment and generally more private and insurance-based solutions. Greater individual assessment of the individual. Lifestyle and health behaviors and other behavioral patterns are monitored for the sake of the public, so that big data can be better planned, and pattern recognition detects it if someone needs guidance on more appropriate behavior. Perhaps citizens' rights will be graduated according to how much they contribute and provide in return. It is no longer considered that rights are automatically something you have simply because you are a national of the country.

The second point she mentioned was the environment. There's going to be a lot more environment. And climate awareness. We have only just seen the beginning of that trend. Meat eaters will be perceived in line with today's attitude towards smokers.

Despite strenuous efforts, only half of the fleet of automobiles has been replaced by electric cars. There are a lot of self-driving cars running in the regular traffic, but there are also still many ordinary cars. A new type of hybrid car has been added that can run both as self-driving and regular cars. Self-driving cars run exclusively in cities.

Many things in the home and daily life are controlled through internet-based technologies. The kind of technology called the internet-of-things. They have finally succeeded in creating an effective firewall so that the internet-of-things can't be hacked, although some believe it makes it a little less smart and user friendly. In return, the authorities have the opportunity to go in and control the functions of people's homes through the internet-of-things if needed. Among other things, the authorities have begun to remand suspected criminals in their own homes as a greatly expanded foot-shacking scheme, which also means that all functions in their homes are controlled fairly strictly through the internet-of-things. It is also used against people who are under surveillance and have been caught planning particularly serious crimes. Mainly if they live alone. If they live with a family, the authorities sometimes in the roughest cases rent a one or two-bedroom apartment for them in a general housing estate, and then keep them behind bars and beat there as a kind of mini prison that is controlled through the internet of-things. On the other hand, a large proportion of the places in the old-fashioned prisons have been closed.

On a more personal level, she believes that gender equality will be improved, both in terms of rights and pay. Gender differences are narrowing, even on the purely external level. There is a trend with new gender neutral first names. Clothes become more independent of gender, and it is now completely different factors that determine which clothes people wear. It is generally accepted that there are many more sexes than the two cis sexes and that everyone has the same rights. At the same time, gender tend to be a private matter, with many preferring to keep their gender out of public spaces as far as possible. Many wear the same kind of scarf and long loose-hanging gestures that hide the shape of the body, regardless of their gender. Without it having anything to do with religion, but simply because they do not want to be perceived as gender objects in public spaces.

It was some of a few of the 40-50 areas she has included in her book. It's giving you something to think about, I believe.

Chapter 41

Where it's long since been both Christmas and New Year's Eve before I've moved on with this

What is the matter with me, I asked myself one morning when I came to look myself in the mirror. It wasn't the most encouraging sight. For a month and a half, I haven't had anything done about finishing this manuscript. I thought I was close to succeeding.

Is this all this Christmas stuff that's still bothering me? Well, hey, we're already halfway through February. It's probably the weather and the winter that's bothering me. All these dark and cold days. I live alone again.

Is it the inner winter that mirrors itself in the outer and makes it so overwhelming?

Or is it the other way around?

You can always say so, if you can't think of anything else.

And now I'm actually a little empty of ideas.

And everything else.

Even girlfriends and stuff like that.

I'll just lick the wounds.

What about this valentine's day coming in a minute?

I am just sitting here getting bored and out of sync with everything.

I don't even want to think about that New Year's Eve.

It was totally silly. I'd rather just forget it.

I'm in a position of hunger. And thirst.

And there's not even any more beer in the fridge.

Chapter 42

Where I had better finish this book so I can win that bet.

Now I have to get this stuff finished. I should have done that a long time ago.

But what do you write in the end of a book like this one? I don't know. I think I've done fairly well after all, and if Mona's sister doesn't acknowledge it, I'm going to get angry. Very angry indeed. And one thing I want to point out: this isn't just plain grey and drilling autofiction like so many other books. No, this book is Mercedes fiction, or Jaguar fiction, or Porsche fiction. Choose for yourself. You know what I mean. Anyway, it is something out of the ordinary. Not just the kind of stuff that one can read in so many other books. And if Mona's sister doesn't want to acknowledge it and give me the $1,000 I've won and acknowledge that I could write a book after all, even if she didn't believe it in the first place, then she's just much, much dumber than I thought it was possible for anyone to be. But in some funny way, that would not even surprise me very much.